ENCORE FOR A DREAM

Limelight Theatre, struggling to survive, is temporarily saved when three sisters unexpectedly inherit it. Rosalind, Olivia and Beatrice are captivated by its charm and the loyalty of the company. With no theatrical experience, the girls strive to combine their own careers with working at Limelight — especially with Gil, the dedicated theatre director. However, an ongoing shortage of cash, a disastrous storm and unforseen tragedy threatens everyone's livelihood, while the girls also have to deal with personal emotional turmoil . . .

SHEILA LEWIS

ENCORE FOR A DREAM

Complete and Unabridged

LINFORD
Leicester

First published in Great Britain in 2009

First Linford Edition
published 2010

British Library CIP Data

Lewis, Sheila.
  Encore for a dream.- -
  (Linford romance library)
  1. Theatrical companies- -Fiction.
  2. Theatrical producers and directors- -
  Fiction. 3. Sisters- -Fiction. 4. Love stories
  5. Large type books.
  I. Title II. Series
  823.9′14–dc22

  ISBN 978–1–44480–073–9

T. J. International Ltd., Padstow, Cornwall

This book is printed on acid-free paper

1

'Here we are,' Rosalind said as they arrived in front of the family solicitor's office in Glasgow's St Vincent Street in good time for their appointment.

'I can't imagine why Mr Stoddart wants to see us again,' Livvy said for the umpteenth time. 'I thought Uncle Walter's will amounted to nothing.'

'That's what we were told at the time,' Beatrice stated as she took Livvy's arm to assist her up the stone staircase to the offices. 'That he had no money to leave Mum. Even his house had been sold years before.'

'Mum always said she regretted that his illness made it difficult for us to see him these last few years,' Rosalind offered as she opened the door to Mr Stoddart's outer office.

'Hello,' she said to the secretary sitting behind a formidable-looking black typewriter. 'I'm Rosalind Forsyth. My sisters and I have an appointment with Mr Stoddart.'

'He's expecting you,' the secretary said. 'Come this way, please.'

Was it really six months since they had last been here, Rosalind thought? Their mother had died very suddenly not long after her uncle Walter, who was in fact the girls' great-uncle. Mrs Forsyth was the sole beneficiary of her uncle's will, but Mr Stoddart had told them then that Walter Gillies had left no money. Now it appeared that he needed to see them concerning the will.

Rosalind was apprehensive that her great-uncle might have left some debts, although she hadn't mentioned that to her sisters, as none of them had much money to their name.

Mr Stoddart was a rotund gentleman with a happy, bouncy personality to match.

'Miss Forsyth, Mrs Webster and young Beatrice.' He greeted the girls according to their age and standing in the family. 'Please be seated. My secretary will bring us coffee and biscuits directly.'

He fussed a bit until they were all comfortably ensconced in chairs.

'Are you keeping well, Olivia? When is the baby due?' he asked.

'September,' Livvy replied with a smile.

'Good, good.' His smile was sincere.

'Now to business,' he said, opening a file on his desk. 'It's about the theatre.'

There was a silence in the room and the three girls looked at each other with puzzled expressions.

'Theatre?' Rosalind was the first to recover. 'You mean the old Limelight? But surely Uncle Walter sold that years ago?'

'No, in fact he didn't,' Mr Stoddart nodded. 'It was bequeathed to your mother. And, of course, her estate is to be divided between the three of you.'

Beatrice leaned forward in her chair.

'Are you saying that *we* own a theatre?' Her tone was breathless.

'I am indeed, but please don't get

too excited about it,' the solicitor cautioned. 'It has taken these last six months for your uncle's lawyer to sort out his affairs and it is only now that I can put the facts before you.'

'Although in his latter years your uncle was unable to take part in the running of the theatre, it appears that he made a monthly payment to help the running costs, a factor not included in his will. However, that money ran out a few weeks ago.'

'Does the theatre have financial problems as a result?' Rosalind cut in.

'I'm afraid so. Unless more money is invested in it, the theatre will have to close,' he replied, his face serious for the first time.

'Oh, no!' Beatrice cried. 'That can't be allowed to happen. So many theatres have gone to the wall recently. Soon Scotland will have no places of live entertainment.'

'Don't exaggerate, Bea,' Rosalind said. 'The situation is not as dire as that.'

'Television is taking over, you know that,' the youngest sister continued. 'And theatres are still such a good training ground for actors. I should know . . . ' Beatrice turned to Mr Stoddart. 'I'm an actress, you see. I had no idea the theatre was still in the family. This is absolutely fantastic news.'

Rosalind and Livvy exchanged a quick glance over Beatrice's head.

'We have no money to finance a theatre,' Rosalind said.

'And even if we did, what's the point? We don't want it.' Livvy shook her head.

'I do! And we'll have the money from the sale of the house,' Beatrice pointed out heatedly.

'You are selling the family home?' Mr Stoddart intervened smoothly.

'Yes, it's too big for Beatrice and me, and we plan to buy a flat nearer to where we work,' Rosalind said.

'You plan to buy a flat,' Beatrice interrupted. 'I'd like my share of the sale to pay for drama college fees, but I'm willing to forget that if we have the theatre to support.'

'I was hoping that my share of the money could be put into my husband's new business,' Livvy told Mr Stoddart.

'I see,' he said. 'Unfortunately, the only way that the Limelight can survive is by having regular financial support.'

'Which we are unable to provide,' Rosalind put in briskly.

'Hang on a minute,' Beatrice interrupted. 'Who has been running the theatre in Uncle Walter's absence?'

Mr Stoddart referred again to the file on his desk.

'A Mr Keith Wilson is the present manager, supported by the theatre's drama director, Gil Buchan.' Mr Stoddart had withdrawn a sheaf of papers from the file.

Rosalind pulled her chair closer to the solicitor's desk.

'May I see those?' she asked.

He slid them over the desk to her. The top few pages were the theatre's accounts for the last three months. She ran a practised eye over them. Everything was in order. All the details of the supplies needed to run a theatre balanced against ticket sales. However, the deficit at the bottom of the sheet was clear to see. The theatre had been running at a loss.

Rosalind picked up a sheet bearing the names of the Limelight staff. In addition to the two members of staff already mentioned by Mr Stoddart, there was a long list of employees, some full-time, others part-time, with the appropriate wages noted against each name.

★ ★ ★

Rosalind sat back in her chair, momentarily disturbed. What would happen to all these people if the theatre closed? The human factor put a different complexion on things.

'Would it be possible to find a buyer for the theatre?' she asked the solicitor.

He gave a rueful shrug.

'As Beatrice has said, some theatres are struggling to survive. The effects of the war to begin with, and now the advent of television.'

'You've all forgotten something,' Beatrice burst out. 'This theatre was Uncle Walter's dream.' She turned to Mr Stoddart. 'He lost his wife and only child in the 1920s and decided to put all his energy into building and running this theatre. How can we abandon something that he kept going all through the war and to the present day?'

'I can appreciate all that, Bea,' Rosalind said. 'But this is the 1950s and so many things have changed — and moved on. He wouldn't expect us to try to keep the theatre going if there is no demand for it.'

'Rosalind is right,' Livvy said. 'Take Donald and me. We're just at the very beginning of building up our new business. That's our dream — a future for our child to come.'

'What happens if no-one buys it as a theatre?' Rosalind asked. 'Will the building be demolished and something built in its place?'

'I should imagine that would be the most likely outcome,' Mr Stoddart replied.

'That would be a tragedy,' Beatrice declared. 'I vote we hold on to the theatre.'

'Oh, Beatrice, what can we do with a theatre?' Livvy said. 'We have no idea about running one, for a start. I don't think we should even consider such a notion.'

'What are your feelings on the matter, Miss Forsyth?' The solicitor looked over the top of his glasses at Rosalind.

'I have accounting experience and I see the problems only too clearly.' Rosalind handed over the theatre's accounts to him. 'It appears to have been running at a loss for some time. I can't see it picking up in the near future, either. I don't think we have a choice. We have to sell.'

'I will inform the theatre management of your decision,' Mr Stoddart said diplomatically.

'Rosalind, how can you be so cold and unfeeling?' Beatrice was furious. 'What about the people who work there and all the actors and actresses who perform on the stage? What will happen to them?'

Rosalind accepted her sister's point, but she had to be practical. They would only have the money from the sale of the family home and she had plans for her share of it. But then, hadn't they inherited some kind of responsibility towards the Limelight?

'Actually, Mr Stoddart, I think it is our place to inform the theatre staff,' Rosalind said. 'I think we should visit the theatre and explain our circumstances. Will you arrange that for us, please?'

★　★　★

Rosalind and Beatrice saw Livvy on to the tram which would take her back to

10

the south side of Glasgow, where she lived with her husband, Donald.

The two women then made their way back to Jardine House, the department store where they both worked.

'I think we should talk things over tonight,' Rosalind said. 'I can't think any more about it now; I must get back to the office.'

They parted at the front door of the store, Beatrice making her way to the beauty counter where she worked as a make-up consultant.

Rosalind took the lift to the top-floor offices and went into the room she shared with Muriel, Andrew Jardine's secretary. She dragged off her jacket and flung her bag on to the chair.

'I take it you didn't hear 'something to your advantage',' Muriel commented, lifting her fingers from the typewriter keys' and settling down to hear the news.

'Well, I won't be buying a yacht, but then again I'm not going off to a debtors' gaol,' Rosalind declared.

'That's a relief.' Muriel laughed. 'Mind you, you would have sorted them all out in prison.'

'Actually, though, it's something that's going to be very awkward to sort out.' Rosalind's bounce left her for a moment and she proceeded to tell her friend about the visit to the solicitor.

'Wow! That's a legacy to shout about,' Muriel exclaimed.

'It would be if we could afford it and also knew the first thing about running a theatre.'

'Beatrice is the gal for that,' Muriel said. 'She's been on a stage more times than I've had hot dinners.'

'I reckon she sees it as a wonderful opportunity to advance her career.' Rosalind shrugged.

'Where is this theatre — somewhere in Glasgow?' Muriel was curious.

'No, it's in a small town called Lockhart on the Ayrshire coast.'

'So, it's a seaside kind of entertainment venue, something like the Gaiety in Ayr?' Muriel asked.

'It might be now, but I seem to remember Uncle Walter wanting it to provide an alternative to variety, with emphasis on plays. Mind you, that's going back to before the war when Mum and Dad used to take me, Livvy and Bea there from time to time.' Rosalind sat down. 'But none of us has been back for years. Too busy with our own lives and jobs, I suppose.'

'Talking of which, old man Jardine wants to see you as soon as possible,' Muriel said.

Rosalind gathered up her notebook and left to see Andrew Jardine. 'Old man' was Muriel's name for him, but, in fact, at approaching forty, he was only a few years older than Rosalind.

On being demobbed from the WAAF thirteen years earlier, she'd found a job in the department store, working for the chief accountant. It hadn't taken long for Andrew Jardine to realise that she had an excellent head for figures and he'd promoted her to be an accounts assistant, with direct responsibility to him. The title was meaningless, typical of the attitude that women didn't hold important posts.

'Sometimes I could scream when I see all these young lads coming into the firm and being promoted to positions of responsibility when I could do their jobs just as well, if not better!' she'd complained to Muriel one day, storming up and down their office. 'They know nothing about working as a team, either. When I was in the WAAF, serving as a plotter, we had to think of all the people whose lives depended on us.'

'You really miss those days, don't you, Ros,' Muriel had sympathised.

'Don't miss the war — glad that's all over — but it hasn't been easy being back in Civvy Street and not getting very far,' she'd said. 'My sisters don't really understand what it's been like and, of course, they think I'm just a bossy boots because I'm the eldest. But I have to take some responsibility as both Mum and Dad have passed away.'

'Beatrice is only twenty-two, isn't she?' Muriel had asked.

'Yes, and Livvy is twenty-four.' Rosalind had given a rueful laugh. 'I'm sure they think I'm ancient at thirty-four.'

Rosalind went into Andrew Jardine's office. It was a rather grand affair with wood-panelled walls and portraits of past Jardines adorning them. Jardine House was a long established family firm and, at the moment, Andrew was the last of the line, as he was unmarried.

'Everything go all right?' he asked, motioning her to take a seat.

Rosalind nodded.

'Just sorted out a few matters.' She had asked only for a long lunch hour to visit the solicitor, but had not told him any details.

'Well, I've had another success.' He moved swiftly on to his own business. He ran a hand over his greying hair, a gesture Rosalind knew he made for comfort rather than vanity. His sober personality made him appear older than his years, but now he was in jubilant mood.

'I've been able to buy Semple's store for a good few thousand less than the asking price. I'm so glad you spotted the monetary flaws in their presentation. You're worth your weight in gold, Rosalind.' He beamed.

But not worthy of a senior position, she thought wryly.

'So, there will be a nice little bonus in this for you.' Andrew Jardine tapped the side of his nose. 'Just keep it between the two of us.'

'Thank you,' Rosalind murmured. Even worse, no public acknowledgment of her business acumen. Much as she liked Andrew Jardine, she could have thrown her notebook at him then.

How long could she sit on her hands and keep her mouth shut? It was all so frustrating. She knew she could achieve much more, but the way ahead for women was blocked by out-dated tradition and lack of foresight on the part of employers.

She was aware that her restlessness was beginning to show itself to Andrew and knew she would have to do something sooner or later. She would write to her boyfriend, Nicol Mitchell, who was working over in Canada as a construction engineer, and tell him about her feelings of unrest, and the Limelight.

★ ★ ★

At six o'clock Rosalind and Beatrice left Jardine House and made their way to Glasgow Central Station to catch the train to the south side of the city.

Together they prepared their evening meal and, after it, sat down to chat.

'I can't wait to see the theatre,' Beatrice began. 'You know, Rosalind, this could be such an opportunity for all of us.' She saw Rosalind's sceptical look and carried on. 'Why don't we try to keep it going and set it up as a repertory theatre? That's what Molly

Urquhart did when she opened Rutherglen Repertory Theatre. She had very little money but everyone pitched in and it became a success.'

'She was able to devote all her time to it,' Rosalind pointed out. 'We have jobs and need our wages to live.'

'But running the theatre *would* be jobs for us,' Beatrice ran on. 'Just think of all the stars who got their start in rep. Duncan Macrae, Stanley Baxter . . . '

'Yes, I know all about that, Beatrice, and I'd love it for you, but you're doing so well in the amateur groups. When any Glasgow company needs someone with your talents for singing and dancing and comedy, you're the girl they ask for,' she said encouragingly.

'But it isn't enough. I want to break into professional acting, on the stage, or the radio. I haven't the experience for television yet,' she admitted.

Rosalind smiled softly. Beatrice not only had ambition but also the sense of purpose that was so important to achieving it. A good proportion of her wages from Jardine House went towards singing and dancing lessons and she was learning the craft of make-up at the beauty counter in the store.

She also had the wonderful gift of mimicry which made her a natural comedienne. In her heart, Rosalind knew that all Beatrice needed was the big breakthrough, but she doubted if that would be at the Limelight.

'I have a feeling that the theatre could be a little run-down,' she said, trying to let Beatrice down gently. 'Please don't pin your hopes on it . . . '

★ ★ ★

Earlier, Livvy had left the tram in Cathcart and made her way to the yard where Donald was working in the garage. He came out to greet her.

'Did it go all right, my dear?' he asked, leaning over to kiss her on the cheek, wanting to hug her but the oil and grease on his overalls would have stained her coat badly.

'Bit of a surprise, love, but I'll go and make tea and tell you all about it.' She gave him a tender smile and went upstairs to the flat above the garage.

Although tiny, the flat was their very own place and both she and Donald treasured it. She knew Donald felt it was rather basic for their needs, but it was their first home and they were both of the same mind. All things had to be earned.

Donald had been working most of the afternoon on his new coach. He'd bought it second-hand from a bus company and had assured Livvy all it needed was the engine tuning up.

His father had set up a travel business after the war and Donald had gone to work for him straight from school. Now his father had offered him the opportunity of running the touring coach side of the business.

Donald had been delighted to get out of the office and, using the engineering skills he'd learned at evening classes, and being a proficient driver, too, he was enthusiastic about the opportunity. With their savings, he and Livvy had bought the garage plus flat. He wanted them to be independent.

When he came upstairs, Livvy set out buttered scones which she'd made that morning and then told him about the surprising legacy.

'That's taken the wind out of my sails completely,' he said. 'I never knew of this theatre's existence.'

'We'd all forgotten about Uncle Walter's Limelight,' Livvy said. 'That's why I never mentioned it. But it's still there and it's now ours and we have a real dilemma of what to do with it.'

'That's the last thing you need, my love,' Donald said quickly. 'You have quite enough to think about what with the baby and the help you've been giving me with the paperwork for the coach business.'

'Oh, I love all that, Donald, and it means we're doing this together.' She smiled as he reached over the table and took her hand. 'That's what marriage is about, sharing and being together.'

'Nearly a whole year now,' he said softly. 'Best year of my life.'

'And mine. I just wish . . . '

'What, Livvy?'

'I thought that maybe Great-uncle Walter had left us some money, after all, and we could have put it into the business. Never mind, we'll have my third of the family house sale.'

'Livvy, you know I want you to keep that money for yourself,' Donald said earnestly.

Since their marriage, she had discovered that he had a strong sense of pride and she had to tread delicately.

'I'll bank it for a rainy day,' she compromised for the time being.

★   ★   ★

He led her from the table to sit on the settee. 'What do you have to do to sort out this theatre business?' Donald asked.

'The three of us have to decide what

happens to it. That worries me,' she told him.

'You didn't ask for this legacy,' Donald pointed out. 'Can't a solicitor sort it out for you?'

'He said he would, but Rosalind felt we should speak to the theatre staff ourselves. She thought it was our responsibility.'

'But what is the point of that? None of you wants a theatre, do you?'

'Beatrice does.' Livvy smiled.

'Much as I admire Beatrice, she doesn't have a business head on her shoulders. If she had that as well as being a good actress, then it would all be different. But the whole things sounds like a white elephant to me.' He shook his head.

'What concerns me is that all the staff will lose their jobs when the theatre is sold.' Livvy sighed. 'How do we face them all and tell them that?'

'You didn't get the theatre into this situation, so you can't be held responsible. To be honest, Livvy, this theatre is of no use to any of you, including Beatrice.'

She nodded.

'Rosalind's opinion exactly.'

'And you, in your condition, certainly don't need this burdensome task of telling the staff.'

'That's true. I dread the thought of going to the theatre and facing everyone,' she admitted. 'I'm no good at that sort of thing.'

'Then don't go. Rosalind is more than capable of handling this and she wouldn't expect you to upset yourself at this time,' he assured her.

'Do you think so?' But in the back of her mind, Livvy was so glad to be relieved of the task.

'Of course, and I couldn't bear it if you made yourself ill over this daft theatre business.'

Livvy laughed.

'Oh, Donald, what would I do without you?'

'Keep me, forget the theatre.' And he bent to kiss her.

★ ★ ★

Later that evening after their discussion, Beatrice asked Rosalind if it would be all right if she went out for a couple of hours. She had promised to meet Stuart.

'A rehearsal tonight?' Rosalind asked.

'No, not tonight. Actually, we're just going to meet at the café. We have some things to discuss.'

'It's fine by me,' Rosalind said, then added, 'Don't be too late.'

Beatrice promised she wouldn't be. Rosalind knew Stuart Cochrane, as Beatrice had brought him home on several occasions, and she rather liked him. He was an electrician by trade and masterminded the lighting of amateur theatre stage shows in his spare time.

Beatrice had met him during a production of 'Oklahoma!' and found they laughed at the same jokes. After that, they began to bounce comedy ideas off each other but had recently become much closer, and Beatrice was alive with excitement as she hurried along the road.

He was already seated in a booth at the Tivoli Café when she arrived. As ever, the table in front of him was littered with sheets of paper.

'Any luck?' she asked, slipping into the booth beside him.

He raised his head in surprise, pushing his glasses up on to his forehead.

'Bea, I'm sorry, I didn't notice you come in,' he apologised.

'Not much of an entrance then. Must try harder.' She sighed.

He leaned over and lightly kissed her cheek.

'You're a show stopper. Don't forget that.'

'Chance would be a fine thing, but tell me your news first,' she replied.

'None of my scripts has been returned yet but I don't know whether that's good or if the comedians are flooded with material.' Stuart flicked through some papers on the table.

Although Stuart's main contribution to the shows was to manage the lighting, his real ambition was to write comedy scripts. When not in the theatre, or at work, he wrote and sent off material to actors and comedians such as Jack Milroy and Jimmy Logan, hoping they'd want to use his sketches and gags. These stars needed a constant supply of fresh scripts.

'Have you sent anything to the BBC?' Beatrice asked.

'Funny you should say that. I wrote this last night for you. It might work on radio,' he said, shuffling through the scripts again. 'It needs a posh voice — Morningside or Kelvinside, take your pick.'

'Oh, Ay can do ayther any time,' she retorted, rolling the words round in her mouth.

'I reckon you're the next Molly Weir.' He laughed.

'I wish,' Beatrice murmured and began to read over the script, noticing how cleverly Stuart had built up to the punchline. He'd written a couple of pantomimes, which had been per-formed by amateur groups, and she'd had the part of June McSpoon from Troon in one and it had been a riotous success.

'Of course, it almost might work as a single spot in a stage show,' Stuart said.

'It's a great sketch and I love it,' Beatrice enthused. 'It would be a dream to perform and you're right about a stage show.'

'You really think so?' He was delighted with her response.

Beatrice sighed.

'And you're not going to believe what I'm about to say . . .' And she told him about the Limelight.

He listened in stunned silence.

'So you're going to have to give it up,' he finally responded when she told him she and her sisters didn't have the money to support it.

'At first I said I wasn't going to sell my share, but I see now that's completely selfish of me. Neither

28

Rosalind nor Livvy can see their way to supporting it. We just don't have the money.'

Stuart took her hand.

'Oh, Bea, that's so disappointing for you. It would have been such an opportunity.'

'For both of us,' she cried. 'If I could keep the theatre I would put on your pantomimes and sketches and we'd both be famous!'

'I've a long way to go. I'm only amateur status at the moment, but I'm never going to give up,' he told her.

'Neither of us is going to give up. I reckon we'll make it one day, by hook or crook, or more likely hard work and a ton of luck!' She squeezed his hand. 'Now, I'm going to throw parsimony to the wind and buy us knickerbocker glories!'

★ ★ ★

Mr Stoddart had written to Rosalind advising her that the theatre staff would

29

be pleased to see the sisters on Saturday afternoon as there was no matinée that day. They were also invited to be present at the theatre's evening performance.

As soon as Rosalind had received the letter, she and Beatrice had gone to visit Livvy and Donald.

'Would you mind terribly if I didn't come with you?' Livvy said.

Rosalind smiled.

'No, of course not. It could be a long and tiring day and I don't want to inflict that on you.'

'It is going to be difficult telling the theatre staff that you can't keep the Limelight going.' Donald said.

'Yes, I'm not looking forward to that,' Rosalind said tentatively. 'But there's something else I want to discuss with you all. It doesn't look as if anyone will buy the Limelight as a going concern, so it seems certain everyone will be out of work.'

'It occurred to me that they probably don't have pensions and, therefore, I wondered what you thought about giving the proceeds of the sale of the theatre to be divided among the staff as compensation?'

'That could soften the blow,' Donald commented.

'It means, though, that none of us will have any money from the sale,' Rosalind pointed out.

'We didn't expect any money from Uncle Walter's will, so I don't see that we're losing anything,' Beatrice said.

'I thought you wanted to keep the theatre going?' Livvy looked surprised.

Beatrice smiled.

'Oh, I do, but I can see that we can't possibly subsidise it. So I reckon we should think of the staff.'

'Yes, I agree,' Livvy said.

'Well done, girls,' Donald declared.

★　★　★

On the way to Lockhart on Saturday, Rosalind broached the subject concerning the sale of the family house with Beatrice.

'Mr Jardine is going to pay me a bonus for my work over a recent transaction,' she said. 'With that and the money from the house I can afford to buy us a flat. And I'd like it if you used your share of the money to train at drama college.'

She put up her hand as she saw Beatrice about to protest.

'I really believe in your talents, Bea. I know if we could keep the theatre going it would be ideal for you. But we can't, and this might help make up for it.'

She glanced at her sister when there was no reply.

'Beatrice, your make-up will be ruined if you don't stop crying.'

They arrived at Lockhart just after lunchtime. It had a small station and they were the only two passengers to leave the train. The May sunshine was glinting off the sea when they emerged from the station. They made their way to the town square.

'Oh, look at that!' Beatrice exclaimed when they spotted the Limelight.

Rosalind hadn't remembered much about the theatre as it was many years since she had visited, and she was now quite overwhelmed by its appearance. The afternoon sun lent a warm glow to the sandstone building and the bow windows placed either side of the classical entrance glinted enchantingly.

'It's like a fairy tale,' Beatrice enthused. 'It would be criminal to knock it down.'

A poster by the front door advertised the current play: *'Mary Rose' by J.M. Barrie*.

'Oh, that's a marvellous play,' Beatrice said. 'The character of Mary Rose goes to a Hebridean island and all kinds of things happen and in the end she's a ghost. I've always wanted to play that part.' She sighed.

As they approached the theatre entrance, a man emerged. He had a business-like look on his face and didn't appear particularly welcoming. Rosalind hadn't expected anything else but she felt uncomfortable.

'I take it that you are the Misses Forsyth?' he said.

'Yes, I'm Rosalind and this is my sister, Beatrice. Our other sister was unable to come with us. She is indisposed.' She thought that was the most tactful way to put it.

'I'm Keith Wilson, theatre manager.' He nodded, and Rosalind didn't offer her hand, suspecting he would think it an empty gesture. 'Please follow me.'

She turned to look at Beatrice and saw the taut expression on her face. This was going to be quite an ordeal for both of them. Would it offend the staff's pride when they offered them the sale money? Rosalind really had no idea if it was the right thing to do.

* * *

They crossed the foyer and entered the theatre proper, following Keith Wilson down the centre aisle. Ahead, Rosalind could see a line of people, backs to the orchestra pit, waiting to meet them.

Her stomach was knotted with nerves.

She steeled herself to remember names as Keith Wilson began the introductions with the man standing on the far right.

'Gil Buchan, theatrical director.'

He was a tallish man, with dark hair and deep blue eyes, and was dressed in a blue pullover and baggy corduroy trousers. He gave her a wary nod.

Next was Jock Simpson, the stage manager. He was small and wiry and it looked as if the lines on his face might crease into laughter, but not today.

Polly Anderson, the wardrobe mistress, was plump with fiery red hair, dressed in purple and equally unsmiling.

The rest of the introductions became rather a blur as Rosalind strove to remember not only names but their roles in the backstage team.

They came to the end of the line and complete silence fell.

'Right,' Rosalind said with a firmness she was far from feeling. 'I'm glad to meet you all and thank you for being such a loyal company for the Limelight. I'm sure our great-uncle Walter would have appreciated all you've done for the theatre over the years.'

No-one reacted at first and she thought she'd have to plough on, then Polly Anderson stepped out of the line. Her determined expression suggested she was about to throw a challenge to the sisters.

'Would you like to see round the theatre since you haven't been before?' she said.

'Oh, but we have,' Beatrice burst out. 'We came with our parents before the war, but I was just little then, so I'd love to have a look around.'

Polly couldn't conceal a look of surprise.

'Please follow me,' she offered.

★   ★   ★

Polly led them on to the stage then through the wings to backstage. Naturally, she started with the wardrobe and

Rosalind was astounded to see the range of costumes, from up-to-date fashion, to Victorian and Regency outfits.

Next they visited the prop store stocked with pieces of furniture from several eras, then they looked in on the laundry room, the scene dock and dressing rooms.

Rosalind noticed that everywhere was meticulously clean, but paint was flaking here and there and the linoleum was well worn.

Eventually they returned to the stage where the rest of the staff were sitting on the furniture of the 'Mary Rose' set. Keith Wilson, however, was situated in the stalls. Rosalind wondered if he was making a point, distancing himself from her and Beatrice.

Rosalind looked directly at Gil Buchan.

'How is this current production doing?'

'Breaking even,' he said. 'But it is a classic play and a tradition that Mr

Gillies was keen to continue alongside the more popular variety shows.' He paused. 'And, of course, he always insisted that we present the amateur shows of the various groups in the area.'

'Oh, I'm all for amateur groups,' Beatrice said. 'They make such an important contribution to theatre.'

No-one replied. Rosalind knew perfectly well that they had assumed the Forsyth sisters wouldn't have a clue about theatre.

Rosalind looked out into the auditorium. Red plush seats, gold flock wallpaper on the walls of the stalls and circle, painted walls in the 'gods', and ceiling chandeliers. It must have been very grand at one time, but now it had a distinctly shabby look.

Clearly there had been no money for redecoration, neither front of house nor backstage.

She was aware of Gil Buchan studying her and knew at once he guessed her thoughts.

'How many productions are already

booked?' she asked him.

'Just three. We decided we couldn't book further ahead until . . . until we knew,' he said in a flat tone.

It struck her that all the money had been invested in productions, and that, after all, was what theatre was all about. She was conscious that the company, although scattered about the stage, all seemed linked by an invisible bond. They were in this together and possibly had been all their working lives.

She was suddenly reminded of her days as a plotter in the WAAF and how the camaraderie had made life bearable even in the face of danger.

Her heart began to race a little as she realised she felt empathy with the people in front of her.

She began to consider if it was possible that with some money the theatre could run for a little longer. Were there any corners that could be cut out of the budget? She'd only taken a cursory look at the accounts in Mr

Stoddart's office. Maybe she could find a way to balance the budget more favourably . . .

The nerves in her stomach were replaced by a tremor of excitement as she mentally added the bonus from Andrew Jardine to the share she would have from the house sale. She could rent a flat for herself and Beatrice, instead of tying up all the money in a purchase.

Livvy wasn't expecting anything from the sale of the theatre and Beatrice could still go to drama college.

Rosalind breathed deeply.

'Beatrice, I wonder . . . ' she began.

Beatrice slowly turned her head, and when she saw Rosalind's face, her eyes lit up.

Butterflies were now whizzing around inside Rosalind and she guessed she was being carried away with the emotion of the situation, but she couldn't stop herself. It was madness, a crazy risk, but above all she knew she wanted to be part of the Limelight.

She linked her arm through Beatrice's and they turned to face the staff.

'Well, now that we've been shown around the place, I expect you are all wondering what our plans are for the Limelight?' Rosalind took another deep breath. 'I'm delighted to say we'll keep the Limelight going as long as we can.' She smiled and tried to take in the reactions.

Gil Buchan was nearest to her and she saw bewilderment upon his face as well as shock, and surprise on the faces of the others.

Beatrice squeezed her arm and Rosalind felt like a weight had been lifted from her shoulders. But she knew in her heart the real work was about to begin.

2

In fifteen minutes, the curtain would rise in the Limelight theatre for the last performance of 'Mary Rose'.

'Three shilling seats, the best in the house,' Beatrice whispered to Rosalind as they took their places in the centre circle. 'Well, after the boxes, that is. I'm glad you didn't take up Keith's offer to sit in one of those.'

'I would have felt I was in a goldfish bowl, and anyway, it's more fun if we're part of the audience,' Rosalind said, one ear cocked to the chatter from the theatregoers around them.

'Have you heard the rumour that the theatre might close?' the lady sitting directly beside Rosalind said to her companion.

'Oh, no! That would be a disaster,' a male voice replied. 'The Limelight is an institution in Lockhart. It's such a wonderful place to come, and besides, the whole community benefits from it. We must do something — get up a petition or whatever.'

Rosalind felt a sense of relief at her decision. The theatre clearly had loyal local support. That would help.

The buzz from the audience was increasing in volume as the seats filled up. Rosalind noticed that everyone had happy, eager expressions on their faces, anticipating an evening of magic, away from the normal routine of life. Just as she was.

The plush on the seats might be a little worn, the ornate ceiling could do with a lick of paint, but none of that affected the sense of anticipation in the air. This was live theatre, it was happening now and the audience wanted to be part of it.

There hadn't been time for a reply from her boyfriend, Nicol, in Canada, but Rosalind decided to write again and tell him the sensational news. Once he was back home she'd bring him here.

He'd just love it.

'Boy, did I learn some stage make-up tips earlier today,' Beatrice said. 'I can't wait to try them out on myself. And what about those costumes? Polly said that wasn't all their stock. Her assistants keep some gowns at their homes. I had a go at painting some flats, too — that's the scenery background, you know, walls and doors . . .'

Rosalind laughed.

'I'm not entirely ignorant, although it's been something of a revelation to see the 'works' as you might say.'

She thought back to that moment on the stage — was it only a few hours ago? — when she'd made the announcement to the company that they weren't going to sell the theatre. There had been absolute silence on the stage for a few moments, as if time was suspended and then suddenly everyone burst into life. Without ceremony, Polly flung her arms first round Rosalind, then Beatrice.

'You can't imagine what this means to us,' she said, emotion making her voice tremble as she dashed some tears from her eyes.

Jock took Rosalind's hand and pumped it up and down until she thought her wrist might give way.

'You're a fine pair of lassies,' he said, his voice sounding rough with relief. 'The Limelight has been my life and I can't imagine how I'd exist without it.'

All the company made a point of speaking both to her and Beatrice — even Keith Wilson, who'd been a little detached earlier.

'Thank you for what you've taken on,' he said. 'Frankly, we were all in a state of despair.'

For a second, Rosalind wavered at the word 'despair'. Had she promised them too much?

Gil Buchan's words were simple.

'Thank you.' They were accompanied by a genuine smile and an admiring expression in his eyes. 'A courageous decision.'

He had pinpointed the essence of the problem. She would need all her courage to cope with this situation and not let the company down.

Polly took charge thereafter.

'This is now your theatre, time for you to see it in all its glory.' She strode off the stage, her purple outfit streaming behind her like a colourful comet. Beatrice was right on her heels.

Rosalind caught Gil's eye.

'I'd go, if I were you. Polly is a law unto herself,' he said, laughing.

It was like entering a different world as Polly described the inner workings of the theatre. Rosalind was first of all struck by the cavernous aspect of backstage. She craned her neck to look up at the 'flies', while Jock was at her side, pointing out the scene dock behind, with its store of flats and benches for the carpenters and painters.

Jock kept up a running commentary on everything, and while it was impossible to take in all at once, Rosalind felt an unexpected thrill coursing through her as she began to understand some of the enormous work involved in presenting a stage show.

★   ★   ★

'Isn't the Star dressing room just tremendous?' Beatrice now remarked.

Rosalind nodded, remembering going down to the theatre basement. The door with the star on it had been open, ready for that night's leading actress. It wasn't large but the huge mirror, with all the light bulbs framing it, had 'Good luck' cards stuck into the edges.

The dressing-table was littered with make-up and powder puffs, while a couple of dresses were hanging from a hook. Another held a hat, and a chair was home to some carelessly flung shawls. It wasn't just an empty room with clothes and accessories. It was an exciting place just waiting for something to happen.

'Gosh, Bea, it must be so thrilling getting ready for a performance,'

47

Rosalind said, shifting in her seat.

Beatrice looked at her over her programme.

'You bet. I can feel my toes tingling now and I'm not even in the show!'

They'd landed in wardrobe next, with its rails of dresses and evening suits and hamper upon hamper of costumes, and Rosalind's doubts about her decision receded as she felt drawn into the whole complex and intoxicating business of being part of a performance.

Every member of the company had a role to play, not on stage, but support for the cast in making sure everything ran smoothly. It must feel like something of a privilege to be part of that.

Gil had taken over then and, having left Beatrice in make-up, he and Rosalind toured the rest of the theatre together.

It was all too much to take in during one afternoon. She wanted to come back by herself to get to know this theatre, to absorb all its history and magic.

* * *

'Here's Gil come to join us,' Beatrice whispered as the safety curtain was raised.

Rosalind smiled as he took the seat next to her. He was a perceptive and kindly man and the future of the drama shows would continue to be in safe hands.

'Are there any members of the Limelight's company not present just now?' she asked.

'None of the part-time staff is here,' he said.

'I'd like to meet them. Would they come to a performance?'

Rosalind turned to Keith, who had joined them momentarily.

'No charge for seats, if that is all right with you.'

Keith laughed.

'Yes, of course. You're the boss.'

For a moment she had the distinct feeling that Keith was relieved to be shelving his responsibility. Had it all been rather a burden to him?

At that moment the safety curtain rose and Keith strode on to the stage.

'Ladies and gentlemen,' Keith addressed the audience. 'As you know, this is the last performance of 'Mary Rose' for the present, but we hope to welcome the Saltoun Players back at a later date.'

'However, tonight we have a reason for celebration but I intend to keep you in suspense until the curtain falls. Enjoy the show!'

The Players put on a flawless performance and Rosalind could tell from the hushed atmosphere in the auditorium that the audience was riveted. Beatrice, practically on the edge of her seat, was transfixed.

'I can't wait until I'm down there acting in front of everyone,' she whispered.

There would be no stopping her now, Rosalind thought, and vowed to herself that if she could possibly manage it, she'd pay her sister's fees at drama college.

While the performers were still on stage after taking their bows, Keith appeared in the orchestra pit.

'You have all been loyal theatregoers of the Limelight and may have been aware of the financial problems we've encountered recently,' he said to the audience.

'However, the great news is that the theatre is not closing, thanks to the support and enthusiasm of the owners, the Misses Forsyth, the great-nieces of our founder, Mr Walter Gillies.'

There was wild applause, stamping of feet and a few whistles.

'Well, now, that's just dandy,' Rosalind heard the man behind her comment. 'I remember Mr Gillies. If these lassies are cut from the same cloth, the Limelight will be in safe hands.'

★ ★ ★

Livvy watched Donald tap the clock on the mantelpiece.

'I know they're late,' she said. 'But they did telephone to say they'd stayed overnight in Lockhart.'

'Whatever for?' he asked, now walking over to the window. 'That must have prolonged the agony all round.'

Livvy picked up the shawl she was crocheting. Almost finished, it had been a joy to make. At that moment the doorbell rang and Donald went to answer it.

'Oh, Livvy, Donald, we had such a wonderful time,' Beatrice said, rushing in. 'You should just see the theatre — it's divine.'

Livvy smiled. Beatrice loved to act, even when it was just the family. Divine, indeed, she thought. An old, run-down theatre!

'You'd think a barn with a platform was great,' Livvy said, then caught sight of Rosalind's face. It was wreathed in smiles.

'Oh, but this was special,' Rosalind said, a touch breathlessly.

'What do you mean?' Livvy began to

feel uneasy. What had happened at Lockhart?

'It's a magical place . . . ' Rosalind began.

'Steady on, Ros, you have told them that it *must* be sold?' Donald interrupted.

Livvy saw Rosalind take a deep breath and knew at once.

'You haven't . . . you didn't . . . ' she gasped, unable to complete the question.

Beatrice danced round the sofa.

'We've told the company we'll keep it going.'

'What?' Donald's voice trembled with shock. 'Rosalind, have you lost your senses?'

With amazement, Livvy saw her older, always responsible, sensible sister smile and then shrug.

'We can't work miracles, but I just know we can do something.' Rosalind sat down close to her. 'I can't explain it, but it felt as if it's been waiting for us to come to the rescue!'

'But Ros, there is no money.' Livvy was horrified at her sister's carefree attitude.

'Well, there is some — a bonus I've been given by Jardines that will keep it going until it's on its feet again,' Rosalind told her.

'This is sheer madness, Rosalind.' Donald obviously could contain himself no longer. 'I have to speak plainly. You may be very good at your job at Jardines, but you haven't the faintest idea about running a theatre, for a start.'

'Pardon me,' Beatrice interrupted. 'We do now! We've inspected every inch of that place and know how it all operates. I learned so much about my profession. I just can't wait to be on that stage.'

Donald, looking exasperated, turned to Rosalind.

'It's not all glamour and fun. Far from it. Running a theatre is a business. You know all the problems Dad and I had setting up the travel agency? And it doesn't end there, we have to keep on top of it all the time. There's cash flow for a start.'

'Donald, there's a manager who's been running it for years,' Rosalind told him. 'He'll keep us on the right lines, especially now that he'll have more money to work with.'

'And when your bonus runs out?' Donald inquired.

Rosalind just smiled at him.

'Believe me, I would never have said we'd take it on if I hadn't . . . ' her voice trailed off.

'If you hadn't been caught up in all the excitement?' Livvy asked quietly.

Rosalind turned to her, smiling.

'Well, yes, Livvy, that was the springboard, if you like. But there's the company to think about. They have been so loyal all those years to Uncle Walter's dream I felt we had to give them a chance.'

Livvy felt flutters of unease. She'd never seen Rosalind like this — dreamy and excited all at once, as if all her practicality had flown out of the window. What if she lost all her money? She sent a beseeching look to Donald.

'I wish I'd come to Lockhart with you,' he said, picking up on Livvy's plea. 'I would have stopped . . . '

'No, you wouldn't, Donald,' Rosalind said calmly. 'Even as soon as I saw the theatre from outside I began to feel it pulling me.'

'Come with us next weekend and see it for yourself,' Beatrice said.

'You're not thinking of investing the family house money in the theatre, too?' Livvy asked, a sudden suspicion crossing her mind.

'For heaven's sake, Rosalind. You'll end up penniless,' Donald exclaimed.

'Donald, credit us with a little more sense.'

Rosalind turned to Livvy.

'Well, there it is, Liv. But it's our decision, Beatrice's and mine. We'll make sure that you don't lose out.'

Livvy shook her head.

'That's not what I'm thinking about. It's you and Beatrice. What might happen if it all goes wrong.'

The sisters didn't stay long. The argument could have raged on but it was not going anywhere.

After they left, Livvy had no heart to take up her crochet again.

'It's absolute madness,' Donald said. 'They'll lose all their money.'

Livvy gazed out of the window, seeing nothing.

'Livvy, you're not to worry about this. Not in your condition. Leave it for a few days, then we'll tackle Rosalind again.'

'Maybe she will see sense by then. Livvy smiled at Donald to reassure him. How she wished Nicol Mitchell was back from Canada. Why didn't that pair get married? It would solve this problem at least. Nicol would see it was a hare-brained scheme.'

★ ★ ★

The phone was ringing as Andrew Jardine opened his office door at

8.15 a.m. on Monday morning. As usual, he was first to arrive, and this morning he felt particularly good. He'd left Jardine House at midday on Saturday and had joined his hill-walking group for a trip to the Highlands. They'd tackled a new Munro yesterday and now he was fit and able for anything.

However, the caller's words on the other end of the phone were a shock.

'I'm sorry. I didn't know you had arranged a meeting for Saturday afternoon,' Andrew responded, flicking open his desk diary at the same time. The page for Saturday was blank.

'You say it was arranged with Rosalind,' he said in answer to the caller's next comment. 'I'm afraid she omitted to tell me ... Yes, I see ... Well, of course you were quite in order to accept the other offer. I can only apologise.' He finished the call.

Andrew was furious. He'd been negotiating the purchase of a warehouse on the outskirts of Glasgow, a property ideal for storage. It was just what Jardine House needed for large items such as furniture.

The seller had called a surprise Saturday afternoon meeting to finalise a quick sale. Andrew knew another store owner was interested and now he'd lost out as the sale had gone through on the spot.

How could Rosalind have made such an appalling mistake?

* * *

'Rosalind! In my office, please.' He called through the open door to his assistant's office as soon as he heard her arrive.

In a small corner of his mind he registered that there was something different about her this morning, but his anger dominated.

'I lost that warehouse,' he began without preamble. 'A meeting was called for Saturday afternoon. One I knew nothing about! Look — there's no entry in my diary. What happened? I need an explanation now!' He pushed the diary across the desk to where Rosalind was standing.

Glaring at her, he saw her visibly pale before him and a hand flew to her mouth.

'Oh, no, how awful. I forgot to tell you about it,' she confessed immediately, and to his consternation she collapsed into the chair on the opposite side of his desk, her hands resting on the diary. 'Andrew, I'm so sorry!'

She looked so stricken that he involuntarily reached out and covered her hand with his. It lay there for a few seconds, long enough for Andrew to recognise this was something he had long wanted to do.

Gently, he withdrew his hand.

'It isn't like you to make a mistake.'

'It was unforgivable of me and now you've lost the warehouse.' Her voice was almost a whisper. 'I think . . . I think I should resign.'

Andrew's anger melted in seconds.

The last thing he wanted was to lose Rosalind. And not only because of her usual business expertise.

'There's absolutely no need for that,' he said. 'It was a mistake, nothing more. There will be other warehouses. What concerns me more is why it happened. Is something worrying you, Rosalind?'

'No. Yes. I'm not sure.'

She looked so distraught he longed to reach for her hand again but decided against it.

'Tell me about it, please,' he said calmly. 'Maybe I can help.'

He listened with mounting alarm to the events of Rosalind's weekend. Clever and astute as she was, he was convinced she had made a huge mistake in keeping on the theatre.

'And I was so caught up with worrying about the theatre and the company, that your Saturday appointment went right out of my mind,' she finished. 'But that's not good enough. My private life should be completely separate from my job.'

Andrew smiled at her.

'Well, let's just say the circumstances were a little exceptional. It isn't every day that a theatre lands in your lap.'

At last she raised her head and he saw a ghost of a smile.

'It was so exciting and thrilling at the time, but now . . . ' She shrugged. 'Maybe I've taken on more than I can cope with.'

'You've given your promise to those people?' he asked.

She nodded but he could see the uncertainty and anxiety in her eyes.

He drummed his fingers on his blotter for a moment, letting his thoughts race ahead.

'I'd like to know more about the Limelight and how it functions. I know nothing about theatres and it's high time I did.'

He was rewarded with a look of amazed interest in Rosalind's eyes.

'As you say, it's your private business so perhaps we could discuss it over a meal, say tomorrow evening?' he suggested.

For a second Rosalind looked completely blank, then she smiled.

'Thank you. I'd . . . I'd like that,' and her voice sounded more positive again.

She left his office and he sat back in his chair, the lost warehouse forgotten. A happy smile played around his lips as he recalled that she'd called him 'Andrew' for the first time.

Was there someone else in her life? He'd heard no office gossip though he'd seen her with a chap at the Kings Theatre one night a few months ago, chatting during the show's interval. But it had looked just like a casual friendship. He found he hoped it was only that.

'You look as if you've had a narrow escape with a Corporation bus,' Muriel commented when Rosalind went into the office.

Rosalind tried to marshal her thoughts and meet Muriel's breezy style.

'I wouldn't call Mr Jardine a Corporation bus, but yes, I've just had a bit of a fright,' she said. Surprise, too, but she had no intention of telling Muriel the private part of her conversation with him. She could still hardly take it in herself.

'I've been on the carpet. Forgot to tell him about an important meeting planned for Saturday and he lost the chance to buy a warehouse.'

'Oh, my stars, what a calamity! Did he give you your books?' Muriel's voice rose a few decibels.

'No, although I offered to resign,' she said. 'It was all because . . . ' and for the second time that morning related the story of her weekend.

'You're never going to be able to do both jobs at the same time, especially since they are in entirely different places,' Muriel remarked matter-of-factly.

'That's true,' Rosalind said vaguely.

Well, she certainly wouldn't let Andrew down again. She was very lucky that he hadn't sacked her on the spot. There had been something different about him, once she'd apologised, but she couldn't quite pin it down.

She was astonished that he was taking an interest in the theatre. And asking her out to dinner! That was not for Muriel's ears, though, as it would probably be wrongly construed.

Rosalind realised her friend was studying her.

'Don't worry, Muriel. I'm not involved in running the theatre, just keeping an eye on it. It will all work out,' she added, her confidence returning by the minute.

★ ★ ★

'You know, Stuart, you look as if you're sulking,' Beatrice said.

Stuart threw the crusts from his sandwiches to the sparrows surrounding their bench in Kelvingrove Park.

'No, just trying to get a word in edgeways,' he replied.

'But you wanted to hear all about the theatre . . . *our* theatre.' She passed him a cup of tea from her flask.

'*Your* theatre in the sticks,' he mumbled.

65

'Stuart! That's unfair and not like you,' Beatrice rounded on him.

'Sorry, but I just know it's going to take you away from me.'

'That's rubbish,' she snapped. 'I'm only going to be there at weekends.'

'But that's when we see each other.'

'Don't worry, I'll be back for the 'Guys And Dolls' rehearsals on Sunday evenings.'

'But we'll both be working then,' he pointed out.

'Well, there's always lunch, just like we're having today.' She was beginning to get impatient with him.

'Stuart — see the Limelight in the long term.' She began to tick off points on her fingers. 'One — I fully intend to get Gil Buchan, the director, to come to see 'Guys And Dolls'. He puts on amateur shows at the Limelight. Why not ours?'

'Two — there could be opportunities for you as a scriptwriter. I did a lot of homework while I was there. The theatre puts on a pantomime and it needs fresh material every year.'

'That's a long shot when I'm a complete unknown,' he said.

'Oh, don't be such a pessimist,' she admonished him. 'We've simply got to seize whatever opportunities come our way and they don't get better than this!'

'It has become the most important thing in your life now,' he said gloomily.

Beatrice linked her arm through his. She couldn't tell him that she saw the Limelight as the place where she'd begin her professional career. He wasn't ready for that yet, but she genuinely hoped he would have success there, too.

'It's just all so new and exciting at the moment,' she said. 'But I have no intention of swapping a theatre for a boyfriend. I love you too much for that.'

★ ★ ★

Rosalind, returning from her lunch break, spotted them walking through Charing Cross on their way back to

Jardine House. Although they were arm in arm, Stuart looked rather woebegone.

She would need to keep a close eye on her sister. While Beatrice would see the theatre as her opportunity, Rosalind wanted her to go to drama school and have proper training. And she knew she'd have Stuart on her side where that was concerned. However, it meant Beatrice would have to stay in Glasgow.

Although her mind felt it was dealing with a hundred different things at once, Rosalind had remembered to search the newspaper for accommodation to let. She crossed the street and greeted her sister and Stuart.

'Hello, you two. I rang Mr Stoddart today. He's put the house on the market and arranged an appointment for us to see a flat at seven tonight.'

'That's great news,' Stuart said at once. 'At least you'll only be at Lockhart at weekends.'

Rosalind immediately picked up on his problem.

'Can you come along with us tonight?' she asked. 'You can keep us right on all matters which need technical inspection.'

'Oh, please say yes, Stuart,' Beatrice said.

His face immediately brightened and he agreed.

'My fees are very reasonable . . . ' he said, laughing.

'Supper later?' Rosalind asked him.

'That'll do nicely,' he said, a wide grin still upon his face as he walked away.

'Thanks, Ros.' Beatrice linked her arm through her sister's as they went in the staff entrance of Jardine House. 'He's a bit put out that I'm going to spend time at Lockhart.'

★ ★ ★

'You're sure you don't mind if I catch an early train back to Glasgow tomorrow morning?' Beatrice asked Rosalind as they unpacked their night clothes in the Lockhart bed and breakfast on the

Saturday afternoon.

'No, of course not. I'm only staying on to discuss the financial arrangements with Keith and Gil.'

'Apart from our rehearsal tomorrow night I can't wait to tell my theatre group about the Limelight,' Beatrice said.

'Don't be tempted to promise them a booking there for your show,' Rosalind cautioned her.

'No, I won't do that.' Beatrice sighed. 'But would it be OK if I asked Gil to come and see our performance in Glasgow?'

'Let's not rush into anything. Gil doesn't know you're interested in acting,' Rosalind reminded her.

That evening in the Limelight, the Lockhart Operatic Society was presenting 'The Mikado'.

'An amateur show and the theatre is almost full.' Beatrice wasn't slow to point out that fact to Rosalind.

'Another full house, almost.' Rosalind passed on Beatrice's observation to Gil as they took their seats in the circle again.

'We like to think of ourselves as a

community theatre with local amateur talent at its backbone.' He smiled. 'Tonight's performers come from all around the area and the audience isn't all family and friends support. The Society has an excellent reputation.'

★ ★ ★

The next day Rosalind had an hour to spare after Beatrice left in the morning and before she met up with Gil and Keith. She took her writing pad from her overnight suitcase and settled down to write to Nicol.

> *Two letters in one week! Sorry I haven't waited to receive your reply to the first one but I simply have to keep you up to date on events. No, what I mean is that I desperately need your usual balanced and objective thoughts on how my life has gone haywire, or so it seems, in the last few days.*
> *Check the address above. Yes, I'm*

at the theatre — which Beatrice, Livvy and I now jointly own! Nearly had to give it up within a couple of days when I made an appalling mistake at work. Andrew J. should have sacked me, but instead has been very supportive. Even took me out to dinner! He's well respected in Glasgow, of course, and has good connections — Trades House, for example. He said he'd look into possible sponsorship!

Meanwhile, house sale is set up and have rented a flat in West End. I can't shake off the feeling that I should be in a circus as I seem to be juggling balls. Wouldn't get a job, though — keep dropping them all.

I feel swept away by all the romance of the theatre and that's so unlike me — unless there's part of my personality I haven't discovered yet? Send a sane letter.

Love, Calamity Jane.

★   ★   ★

Rosalind shared a sandwich lunch with Keith and Gil and complimented them on the previous evening's excellent performance.

'We have some first-rate local amateur groups,' Gil said.

'And some of them come cheap,' Keith pointed out. 'But you can't run shows on amateur talent indefinitely.'

They cleared the plates away and Rosalind spread her papers across Keith's desk.

'I saw the theatre's accounts when we visited our solicitor a couple of weeks ago,' she began. 'I collected them from him this week and have had a really good look at them.'

She looked up to see Keith frowning.

'I work with accounts in my job in Glasgow so I know my way around balance sheets,' she said with a friendly shrug, not wishing to cause offence.

'I think you'll find that everything is in order,' Keith said stiffly.

'In perfect order,' Rosalind agreed at once, regretting that his feathers were ruffled, despite her tact. 'I've instructed my bank to transfer the capital I have to invest into the Limelight account.' And she mentioned the sum involved.

'Wow, that will make a terrific difference,' Gil said at once, a huge grin on his face.

'I wish she'd had this money a few months ago.' Keith was still sounding aggrieved.

'I didn't have this money a few months ago,' Rosalind casually told him. 'I recently received a bonus from my firm. Beatrice and I can probably invest some more when our family home is sold.'

'Your family home?' Gil leaned over the table. 'You can't sell that to help us.'

'We were going to sell it anyway,' Rosalind told him. 'Don't worry, we're not homeless. I'm renting a flat in Glasgow.'

'So what you're saying is that the money you're depositing is all that you can give us?' Keith asked.

Rosalind tried to keep calm.

'Yes, as I've said, at the moment.' She noticed the glare that Gil sent towards Keith. 'At first we felt we had no option but to sell the theatre,' she continued, 'as we don't have sufficient income from our wages to keep it running.'

'Was it only the bonus that made you change your mind?' Keith asked.

'Not at all. I had other plans for that, but when we came here, saw the theatre and met the company with its terrific team spirit it made all the difference. We wanted to be part of it, do what we could to keep it going. We love it!'

'You might love it, but once your money is gone, the theatre goes, too,' Keith said with finality.

Rosalind noticed that Gil's fists were balled on the table, the knuckles showing white. She couldn't understand why Keith was being so difficult. She picked up her pen and drew her papers towards her.

'Goodness, I hope not. I thought we

might work together on some economic possibilities. You can both guide me on those.'

'You mean there's something we've overlooked?' Keith asked, a thread of sarcasm in his voice.

'I think Rosalind means that she's looked at our difficulties and could possibly suggest a fresh approach to dealing with them,' Gil interposed smoothly with a certain firmness in his tone.

'Thanks, Gil, although I don't presume to know better than you two.' Rosalind was treading very carefully now. Keith was a prickly customer. 'Actually, one possibility that occurred to me was a rethink on some ticket prices, such as offering reduced rates to students and retired folks. Other theatres do that.'

'That won't make money, just the opposite,' Keith said with a barely concealed sneer.

'Not if it brings in the customers,' Gil pointed out. 'We could have full houses and balance the books.'

'There are possibly other economies which we could look at,' Rosalind said. 'Should we discuss them now — what do you think?' She noticed Keith glower but Gil was looking interested.

'What I think is that you're saying I've mismanaged this theatre for years.' Keith got to his feet and his voice gradually became louder. 'And if you think that by coming in here with no experience and waving a magic wand will make everything come out all right then you're living in Cinderella land!'

'That's enough, Keith!' Gil leapt up and faced the manager. 'Apologise to Rosalind. She's offering her suggestions, not giving orders.'

'It will be orders soon enough. And I'm not taking them. I've never been so insulted in my life! You try to run this theatre and see how you get on.' He glared at Rosalind. 'My resignation will be in the post tomorrow.'

And he swept out of his office. Rosalind froze with shock. What had she done? How could the theatre run without a manager? Within a week of taking on the Limelight it looked like it might go under after all.

3

Rosalind stared at her hands as she stood in Keith's office. It had taken all her self-control to keep calm in front of Gil after Keith's spectacular walk-out from the theatre.

Now, though, she countered the shock of his announcement by allowing anger to take over.

'How could he do that?' she demanded of Gil. 'I thought we were all pulling together to save the Limelight?'

'We are!' Gil himself sounded angry and, for a moment, Rosalind thought it was directed at her.

'Sorry, Rosalind,' he said after a moment in a calmer tone of voice. 'Please, sit down.'

She hadn't realised she was still on her feet, having jumped up when Keith had suddenly left the office.

'We're all behind you here.' He

paused. 'Keith wasn't so much involved with the theatre as the rest of us, not having grown up with it, as it were.'

'But just to walk out — what will he do?' she asked.

'I think he's been applying to other theatres. None of us was sure if we would have a job for long. He has a young family and had to think of them.'

'I would hate to think I was the reason for his resignation.' Her anger had drained away now.

'I think you gave him a let-out without him losing face,' Gil said.

Even that small sense of relief wasn't enough to lessen the shock. With a tremendous effort, Rosalind controlled her inner panic.

'So, how do we go about getting another manager?' she asked.

Gil had now returned to his chair at the opposite side of the table.

'I could do it,' he said quietly.

'You? But you're the theatre director, concerned with the artistic side of the theatre, not the business.'

'You don't think I'm capable?' His quick answer was accompanied by a dangerous flash in his eyes.

'It's not that, Gil,' she said, spreading her hands. 'I just don't know anything at all about how a theatre runs — as yet.'

'Don't you think that until you do, you need to rely on someone like me?' He gave her a very direct stare.

'That's true,' she said matter-of-factly. 'But I have to ask myself if it is fair of me to put this burden on you.'

Gil relaxed a little and gave her a ghost of a smile.

'It could be a burden. I don't know yet, but I'd like to give it a try.'

'Will you eventually want to move on to a bigger and better theatre?' she asked. She didn't want to be left in the lurch a second time.

His face closed.

'I have no plans to leave Lockhart.'

Rosalind's uneasiness was now directed at herself. She felt as if she'd stepped across an invisible line and the other side was intensely private. Gil had said he had no plans to leave the town, but not the theatre.

'Shall we go for a trial period?' she suggested, thinking that was the fairest option.

His expression was wary, as if he felt he didn't have her full confidence.

'Yes, fine,' he said flatly.

'We can make some adjustments to your salary to take into account — ' she began.

'No need,' he interrupted. 'I don't want more money. I want to keep the theatre going.'

'I'll take care of the accounts — not because I don't trust you,' she said with quick emphasis, 'but accounting is my profession, and I can handle it as well as my job in Glasgow.'

'That's fine by me. That side of the job would take up too much of my time,' Gil said.

Rosalind lowered her eyes. Gil was a far stronger character than his outwardly genial appearance suggested.

She didn't think for one minute it was going to be easy working with him, especially as she had so much to learn. The one fact that was not in doubt was his devoted loyalty to the Limelight. She must never forget that.

'Right,' Rosalind said, anxious to move on and hopefully lessen the tension. 'Tell me what needs to be done in order of priority.'

The tight look left Gil's face to be replaced with an expression of resolve.

'I'd like to have bookings to carry us through the summer.'

'Do you know which companies or shows you want?' she asked.

'I've made some tentative bookings, but now that I know how much money is available, I can confirm those. In fact, I can wrap up the summer season.' He smiled with some satisfaction.

'That's great.' She felt her spirits rise. Things were looking up. 'And after that?'

'I'd like to attract some major talent from Glasgow for the autumn season, which tends to fall off a little,' he said. 'Television is taking off but many actors and actresses like to back up their performances on the screen with live appearances at theatres, so that audiences don't forget them.'

'That's good news for us. Should we see some shows, say in Glasgow?' she asked.

★   ★   ★

He looked at her, surprised. 'That's how I find shows and actors. Do you want to come along, too?'

'How else will I learn what is right for us?'

Again there was that ghost of a smile on his face.

'Once I have the autumn bookings sewn up it will give me time to organise the Christmas panto,' he said.

'Have you a star in mind for that?'

'A couple spring to mind, but I'll have to check if they're available — and then there are their fees!' His voice took on new enthusiasm. 'Panto is also a good way to put new talent on the stage and I might be lucky and find fresh writers for the gags and comedy sketches.'

Rosalind immediately thought of Stuart, but was he ready for that yet? Beatrice considered he was brilliant, but then, that was love for you.

'I take it that you agree with me about revising ticket prices?' she asked.

'Yes. I wanted to change those ages ago but Keith wouldn't agree.' He shrugged. 'If we had, we might have avoided running at a loss.'

Rosalind just nodded, but she felt it was vindication for her stance against Keith.

'We might have to think about the fabric of the theatre. I reckon there's quite a bit of refurbishing needs doing,' she said.

Gil got up from his chair and went over to the office window.

'We can't afford that at the moment,' he said flatly.

'It's not all about shows and actors and scripts.' She tried to tease him a little.

He turned from the window.

'It is for me.'

It was like a gulf yawning before her. Gil's first priority was what happened on the stage and she had to accept that. The responsibility for everything else was now hers. She'd have to do her sums very carefully to see if there was enough money for maintenance. It could be some time before the performances showed a profit.

'I wonder about seeking financial assistance from the community,' she began, thinking of the suggestion Andrew Jardine had made. 'Do you think it would be a good idea to start with an appeal through the local newspaper, for instance?'

Gil gave a casual nod.

'It's worth a try. I know the guy on the 'Lockhart Weekly News'. I'll have a word with him.'

'Thanks, I'd appreciate that,' she said

and stood up, shuffling her papers together.

Rosalind was emotionally and physically exhausted. She and Gil had come to some kind of agreement, but still the atmosphere was a little tense. She had intended to spend more time at the theatre, but now she just wanted to get away and think.

'Let me know what shows you want to see in Glasgow,' she said. 'I'll organise the tickets. Otherwise, I'll see you next weekend.' She smiled at him.

'That's fine,' Gil replied in his normal calm tone, but his face was quite unreadable.

From the moment Rosalind left the office, to the train journey from Lockhart to Glasgow, the seesaw of her hopes seemed to dip down again.

* * *

Gil opened the door to the foyer of the Grand Duchess theatre for Rosalind. Considering it was situated almost in the suburbs of Glasgow, it still commanded good audiences. While it didn't have the glamour of the Alhambra or the King's Theatre, the shows were still top class and actors and actresses vied to perform there.

Rosalind and he had taken in the shows in the major theatres in the past couple of weeks and it had been his suggestion that they come to the more modest one.

'It's Livvy's birthday next week and we're having a small family party,' Rosalind said to him. 'You're more than welcome to join us, Gil. I know that everyone would be delighted to see you there.'

'I'd like that.' He smiled in agreement.

On the business side of things, he'd been impressed with Rosalind's quick grasp of the essentials of staging shows during their visits to the starry theatres. She was trying very hard to acquire an all-round knowledge of theatrical matters. However, she could be prickly and had strong ideas, determination being one of her main characteristics, and he knew it wasn't going to be all sweetness and light working with her.

Beatrice erupted into the theatre foyer with her usual enthusiasm and introduced Gil to her boyfriend, Stuart. Gil shook hands with the young lad. There was an air of excitement about him and he wondered if it was Stuart's first visit to the theatre.

'I missed you at the other two shows,' Gil said to Beatrice.

To his surprise, she flushed and darted a look at Stuart. Almost a warning look, he thought.

'Sorry, we were busy on those evenings. Stuart and I had to see some people,' she said quickly.

It was a lame excuse and Gil thought it was completely out of character for Beatrice, although Rosalind had said the same thing when he'd asked why she wasn't with them to see the previous performance. It was a puzzle, as he could have sworn Beatrice was genuinely interested in the theatre, thinking back to the day when they'd first arrived in Lockhart.

★ ★ ★

He might not understand the sisters very well but, he thought later, it was odd how you could meet someone who was entirely different in personality, occupation and ambition and yet feel as if you had an instant bond with them. So it was with Donald Webster, Livvy's husband.

Livvy herself was charming, her face shining with beauty at this stage in her pregnancy. She made a point of saying how much she appreciated what Gil was doing with the theatre.

'As you know, I'm not involved with it, but Donald and I support the girls all the way,' she said. 'Rosalind has told us about your dedication, Gil.'

Gil hid his surprise. He hadn't been sure what kind of impression he'd made on Rosalind.

Rosalind hurried in just then and produced the tickets. The men stood back to let the ladies start up the stairs to the Grand Circle.

'Aye, we support the girls.' Donald took up Livvy's remark as he and Gil made their way upstairs. 'But I know theatre is a risky business. We can't help financially but I have a proposition that might be fruitful. Maybe we can discuss it later?'

Gil nodded, wondering why Rosalind hadn't mentioned this. He took his seat beside her in the circle but he had no time to ask as the curtain was rising.

* * *

'What do you think of it?' Rosalind asked Gil eagerly at the interval. 'Good production, well staged, but not a show we can afford,' he told her.

'But what of the cast?'

'The two stars wouldn't come to Ayrshire, not at this stage in their careers. They're heading for the big time,' he said. 'But the second lead, Avril Beaton, might consider appearing with us provided she was given a starring role.'

'And what about the young lad, the comedian's feed?' she asked.

Gil turned to smile at her.

'Well spotted, Rosalind. Yes, he's going places. He has a natural gift for timing and uses the stage well. I'll look them up in 'Spotlight' and contact their agents. Of course, it all depends on their availability.'

He heard her sigh.

'Nothing is quite as cut and dried as it seems.'

'No, not like accounts,' he told her.

She gave him a cool look and he could have bitten out his tongue. He hadn't meant it to sound derogatory. She was making such an effort to grasp his side of theatre without his long years of experience. He really would have to try harder to make their partnership work in a more harmonious way, otherwise ... well, it would, as they said in the business, be 'curtains'.

It was as they were saying their goodbyes in the foyer that Donald drew him aside.

'I run a touring coach business, one route being down the Ayrshire coast. Burns Cottage is included and various other points of interest. It might be good business for us both if I included one of your shows at the Limelight as part of the trip.'

'Now that's a great idea,' Gil said at once. 'We could give you good terms on the tickets for a group booking.'

'Smashing. It could also help to publicise the theatre. Our passengers would tell their friends. After all, word of mouth is the best form of free publicity.'

Gil held out his hand.

'You know, it's been great to meet you and Livvy. The whole family is so enthusiastic about the Limelight.'

Donald touched his nose with his finger.

'I'd better be the one to tell Rosalind

about our plan. I just wanted to sound you out first.'

'Sure thing,' Gil said, concealing a smile. Did Rosalind rule the roost in the family? Maybe she was just used to being in charge. However, much as she wanted to learn all aspects of theatre production, he was in charge of that area and there would be no change there.

★ ★ ★

They all went their separate ways outside the theatre. Donald was taking Livvy's sisters home to their new flat in the west end, whereas Gil was making for the station to catch the last train to Lockhart.

'I'll walk with you,' Stuart said to Gil. 'I get the underground down at St Enoch.'

'Did you and Beatrice enjoy the show?' Gil asked as they crossed the street just ahead of a clanking tram.

'Very much, although I thought some

of the gags were ready for a pension,' he said.

Gil laughed.

'Yes, time the show had some fresh material.'

'It's good to watch a professional show, though, to see how it can be done with the right money and equipment,' Stuart said.

'And what did you think of the cast?' Gil asked.

'The stars tried to hog it,' Stuart said bluntly. 'I know I'm prejudiced, but Beatrice can sing and dance better than that June Simson.'

Gil smiled to himself. June Simson was probably the most popular performer in Scotland at the moment.

'It's a pity, then, that the pair of you couldn't come to the two other shows I saw with Rosalind.'

'Well, we were rehearsing,' Stuart said casually.

'Rehearsing what?' Gil asked.

Stuart stopped dead on Argyle Street, looking most embarrassed.

'Oh, heck, I wasn't supposed to say.'

Gil waited, staring at him.

'We were rehearsing 'HMS Pinafore'. Beatrice and I are with the Serenade Singers amateur group,' Stuart confessed.

Gil felt a mixture of excitement and annoyance. He'd heard of this group, although he had not seen them perform yet. Usually he tried to go to amateur performances as well as professional. But why hadn't Beatrice mentioned she was a member of the group?

'Are you and Beatrice taking part in the opera?' he asked.

'I'm just in charge of the lighting, but Beatrice . . . Beatrice is the lead. She's taking the part of Josephine.' Stuart couldn't keep the pride from his voice.

Gil took a deep breath.

'You mean that Beatrice can sing and act?'

'She's always the star of our shows. She's mad about the stage.'

'Has she had any training?'

'Only private lessons so far. Rosalind

wants her to go to drama college.'

'When is the Gilbert and Sullivan performance by your theatre group?' Gil asked.

'Next week. It's on for five nights.'

'Will you get me a ticket for a performance?' Gil paused. 'Oh, don't tell Rosalind or Beatrice that I'll be there. I'll just surprise them.'

Stuart promised him and Gil bid him a hasty goodnight as he had to sprint for his train. Once seated in his compartment he pondered over Stuart's news. If Beatrice was a good enough singer and actress to handle the part of Josephine, then she might have a future on the professional stage if that was what she wanted.

What he couldn't understand was why this hadn't been mentioned when they'd inherited the theatre. Surely Beatrice — and Rosalind for that matter — must have seen the opportunities it offered?

★ ★ ★

For Rosalind, it was a completely new experience to be travelling to Lockhart by car. Although Andrew had said he wanted to see the Limelight, Rosalind had not expected him to visit so soon. However, he insisted on driving her and Beatrice down to Lockhart on the Saturday morning.

Beatrice, who hadn't been to Lockhart the previous weekend on account of taking part in her show, had at first been rather overwhelmed that she was sitting in her boss's car. She was not on the same familiar terms with him as Rosalind.

'And are you settling in to your new abode?' Andrew opened the conversation once they were heading down towards Greenock. He'd told them he would take the coast road so that they could enjoy the views.

Rosalind concealed a smile. Sometimes Andrew could be just a little old-fashioned with his language.

'It's so different from our old house,' Beatrice said, her natural exuberance overcoming her reticence. 'As it's a top floor flat we have this wonderful view over Glasgow. There's the university and the art gallery, then just a glimpse of the River Clyde, with Cathkin Braes on the far horizon.'

Rosalind was more than delighted with the move. The flat was much easier to run and there was less travelling to work for both her and Beatrice. And Livvy now had her share of the money from the sale of the house, which would surely help Donald's business.

'And when is the housewarming to be?' Andrew asked.

'As soon as we are tidy!' Rosalind said, smiling.

Rosalind hadn't thought of a party but it would be a good idea. She'd wait until Nicol was back from Canada. She wanted to straighten out a few things with him and the party would be ideal opportunity to show him exactly how things stood regarding the Limelight. She thought of his last letter, received only the day before.

I just wish this contract was over, he wrote. *I'm missing you like crazy and now I hear you're being wined and dined by stuffy old Andrew. He's never paid you that kind of attention before. What's got into the man — trying to steal my girl . . . ?*

Was that the impression Nicol had taken from her last letter to him? But it hadn't been like that at all. She was sure Andrew's gesture had been a way of apologising for his outburst of temper — even though the situation had been her own fault.

Yet she couldn't deny that there was a subtle change in their relationship as boss and assistant, but surely only because he was interested in her new venture with the theatre, not in her as a person. Nicol was reading far too much into it.

She'd write to him once back in Glasgow and put him right where Andrew was concerned. However, it might be tactful not to mention her boss's presence at the theatre today.

'I'm looking forward to this visit,' Andrew said, looking across at Rosalind in the passenger's seat. 'I was concerned when you told me your manager had resigned. Are things working out?'

'So far, so good. Gil Buchan is taking a lot on his shoulders and I'm trying to keep my end up with the accounts, the wages and so on.' Rosalind made light of the fact that she spent most evenings working on the theatre's finances.

'And is there still enough money in the kitty?' he asked.

'For our present needs, yes,' she said. 'I made an appeal in the local paper for financial support. Gil set up an interview for me with the reporter and it was in last week's edition. I'm hoping there might be some response this weekend. From what I've heard the folk in Lockhart certainly want to keep the theatre going.'

'Good thinking, Rosalind,' Andrew said. 'Get to the heart of the people.'

★ ★ ★

As they drove into Lockhart, Rosalind waited for Andrew's first impression of the Limelight. She wasn't disappointed.

'My word, now that is a beautiful building. It would have been an outrage if it had been sold to developers,' he announced even before he had parked the car.

'Exactly our thoughts,' Rosalind said.

He got out of the car and gazed at the theatre exterior with a critical eye. She remembered his expertise in assessing buildings in Glasgow — those that he hoped to acquire, at any rate.

'It looks to be in sound condition,' he said. 'Well, perhaps the stonework needs some attention. How about the roof?'

'Roof?' Rosalind strained to look up at the top of the building.

'That's usually the first place to sustain any deterioration,' Andrew said portentously.

'I . . . I hadn't thought of that. The interior is a bit shabby,' she admitted.

'Mm . . . The whole place probably

needs a thorough inspection on safety grounds alone. I would attend to that as soon as possible, if I were you, Rosalind,' Andrew said. 'Let's go inside.'

Rosalind's spirits plummeted. She had been looking forward to showing Andrew their inheritance, but already it seemed that new problems had been thrown up.

As they walked down the centre aisle, Rosalind could see Gil on the stage, chatting to a lady. As they grew nearer she recognised her. It was Avril Beaton, the actress they'd seen at the Grand Duchess theatre.

On stage, everyone was briefly introduced to each other.

'So glad to meet you.' Avril clasped Rosalind's hand. 'And I just love your theatre. I always like to check over a place before I commit myself to a show.'

She could only be described as an elegant beauty, Rosalind thought. Taller than she appeared on the stage, with graceful carriage to complement her classic style.

'And what do you think of it?' Rosalind held her breath.

'I can't wait to perform here.' Avril beamed at everyone. 'Gil and I are just discussing possible scripts at the moment. It is so exciting.'

Rosalind caught Gil's eye and he gave her a small triumphant smile. There was no doubt that the appearance of Avril Beaton would bring in a good audience.

'And what part do you play in the theatre, Mr Jardine?' Avril turned her attention to Andrew.

Rosalind was surprised to see that he seemed unable to reply for a moment. He was gazing at Avril with frank admiration.

'Nothing, I'm sorry to say.' The words came out eventually. 'Rosalind is my assistant in Glasgow and I just came to see the family theatre I've heard so much about. I'm afraid I'm just a boring old store owner.'

'No-one is ever boring if they are even the tiniest bit interested in theatre,' Avril told him with a winning smile. 'Let me be the one to show you around.'

Rosalind watched in amazement as Avril slipped an arm through Andrew's and began to lead him off the stage, chatting to him nineteen to the dozen.

'There's something I'd like to discuss with you, Rosalind, about Beatrice, actually,' Gil said. 'Let's go to the office.'

There was a slight constraint in Gil's voice. She looked over to where her sister was talking with a stagehand and debated whether to call her. Then she decided that if Gil had wanted her with them he would have said.

$\star$ $\star$ $\star$

The first thing Rosalind saw when she followed Gil into the office was a pile of mail sitting on the desk, together with the week's copy of the 'Lockhart Weekly News', which contained their appeal for support.

'Oh, my goodness, look at all these letters!' she exclaimed. 'Do you think we've got a good response, Gil? Let's open them now!' She tore the nearest envelope open and a cheque fell out together with a letter.

'Look! A cheque for one hundred pounds. It's from a hotel. The Urquhart Arms.'

She read the letter as fast as she could.

'I can hardly believe it. And they say they'd like us to run an ad for the hotel in our programmes. We can do that easily, can't we?'

'Yes, we must let the printers know as soon as the next programme is due,' Gil said.

'Can you phone them now? The second paragraph gives all the details.' She passed the letter over to him and Gil scanned it. 'I'll phone the hotel and thank them and tell them about the ad.'

Rosalind felt a rising sense of buoyancy. It could be the beginning of a real breakthrough. Another letter was ripped open.

'Oh, that's lovely. The Scouts and Guides are going to give us the proceeds of their jumble sale.' She waved the letter at Gil but he was talking on the phone, though he managed to nod.

Another local company promised to sponsor a show in the future and the local operatic society said they would perform for a week at no charge.

'Rosalind, the printers say there should be a letter from them.' Gil held his hand over the mouthpiece of the phone.

Rosalind scrabbled through the rest of the envelopes until she found one with the printer's name on the back. She ripped it open.

'A reduced price for ticket printing! Thank them so much!'

Gil spoke into the phone again while Rosalind finished dealing with the letters.

'Quite a few promising ones here,'

she told him when he replaced the receiver. 'No more actual cash, but help is offered in kind from various businesses. Redecorating jobs, some new electrical fittings, that kind of thing.'

Gil smiled and tapped the newspaper.

'It was a good idea to appeal.'

'I thought we were taking a chance, but it's proved to me how much the theatre is valued in Lockhart, and how many local supporters there are in the town.' Rosalind paused. 'That's all down to you and the team here. You've obviously carried on Uncle Walter's dream.'

Gratitude and euphoria were surging through her body and she suddenly wanted to hug someone. Gil was smiling at her obvious joy.

'Come on, let's tell everyone the great news.' She turned to leave the office then stopped.

'Gil, I'm sorry. You said you wanted to talk about something to do with Beatrice. Please, can it wait?'

Gil hesitated.

'Yes, OK, in the circumstances. But we have to sort it out soon.'

Rosalind didn't register the underlying tension in his voice as she swept out of the office.

Andrew Jardine and Avril Beaton were back on the stage, chatting to Beatrice, and they had been joined by Polly, Jock and other members of the company.

'Listen, everybody,' Rosalind carolled as she ran on to the stage from the wings. 'We've had loads of support from our appeal. We're riding high for the moment and we can plan some good shows.'

Avril immediately applauded.

'Well done! Let's put the Limelight on the map again!'

Andrew gave her a beaming smile, while Polly, Jock and the others were cheering.

'I want to thank all the Limelight team for . . . ' Rosalind's thank you was interrupted by the sound of a door banging in the auditorium.

★ ★ ★

All eyes turned to look. Striding down the centre aisle was a tall man, a huge smile on his face.

'Rosalind, isn't that Nicol?' Beatrice whispered.

Rosalind was speechless. Nicol was in Canada! But no, he was bounding on to the stage.

'Surprise, my lovely Rosalind. I cut short my contract as I couldn't wait any longer to see you.' With those words he swept her up into his arms.

For a second Rosalind stood stock still, but through the warmth of his arms, mixed with the pleasure at seeing him again, she soon melted into his embrace.

Then, in front of everyone, he kissed her, very soundly but also with great tenderness. It was an entirely new experience for both of them.

She drew away from him, shaken by the sensation but well aware that Nicol had taken advantage of the situation.

He knew only too well that she hated any public demonstration of emotion.

She was immediately conscious of the reaction of the others on the stage. Beatrice had a surprised smile on her face, while Andrew was frowning. For a moment Gil looked puzzled, then he turned away.

'Now that's real romance,' Avril said mischievously.

Rosalind bristled but she could hardly remonstrate with Nicol in front of everyone. Besides, it must have looked as if she had enjoyed every moment of their reunion.

For the first time in her life, Rosalind couldn't work out exactly what her emotions were telling her.

4

The setting sun was sending red streaks across the sky, reflected in the still waters of the Firth of Clyde. The outline of the Isle of Arran was a dusky shadow in the distance, lending an air of romance and mystery to the scene.

Not that the present scene needed any aid to romance, Rosalind thought, as she gazed across the table at Nicol sitting opposite. Somehow he had found this seaside café perched on a hill just outside Lockhart and had brought her here for a quiet meal, away from the bustle of the Limelight.

'Happy, my love?' he asked, touching her hand across the table.

Rosalind smiled at him.

'Gloriously,' she said softly.

At that moment the waitress brought their soup and Rosalind reflected on the amazing two hours since Nicol had unexpectedly turned up at the theatre.

That moment on the theatre stage would live with her for ever. Her initial concerned reaction to Nicol's dramatic arrival had quickly evaporated when he had taken hold of her arm, drawing her round to face him. He had looked at her with such an expression of love and longing that it had completely taken her breath away.

It had also triggered an unexpected response in her that had sent a surge of joy through every nerve in her body. She had been unable to take her eyes from his as she'd tried to control these newly discovered and wonderful feelings. How had their good, solid friendship blossomed into this state of sheer happiness?

Had, in fact, this love been growing and simmering away in the two years that they'd known each other? Had their enforced parting brought this right out into the open?

She didn't care how it had happened, just that it had!

'So, my dear one, how about showing me this wonderful theatre?' he had said softly.

Somehow she'd brought herself down to earth, aware again of all the others on the stage.

She'd squeezed Nicol's hand and then had turned to face everyone.

'Talk about being swept off your feet,' she'd begun with a light laugh. 'And you don't even know who he is! Well, this is Nicol . . . Nicol Mitchell, my boyfriend, who has been working in Canada over these past few months. I didn't expect him home yet and this has all been a bit of a surprise!'

'I'll say!' Beatrice had chimed in. 'Welcome home, Nicol.'

Nicol had gone over to her and had planted a light kiss on her cheek.

Then Rosalind had taken him by the hand and, one by one, had introduced him to everyone on the stage.

★ ★ ★

114

'Oh, no, I think the sun is finally setting,' she cried as she put down her soup spoon and gazed out of the window as the red streaks faded from the sky.

'Oh, it will be up again in the morning,' Nicol said with a wink. 'Just think, a new day . . . a new beginning,' he said with significant meaning.

'I'm so glad you're back with me,' she told him. 'I've missed you so much.'

'I just wish I could have been with you over the business of the theatre and all the work you've had to do. I had no idea you'd taken on so much.'

She smiled at him.

'I tried to keep my letters casual and funny. I knew you would have worried far too much.'

'I worried anyway,' he said softly. 'Worried that you might be overworking, that your train home might not arrive on time, that it might rain and you'd forgotten your umbrella.'

'Oh, Nicol.' She laughed. 'That's very sweet.'

'Only because I love you, Rosalind.'

'As much as I love you?' she teased.

'You do? Really?' His voice was low.

She nodded.

'I wasn't sure,' Nicol said. 'We'd never said anything before . . . but I hoped.' He leaned across the table and clasped both her hands in his. 'My love is for ever!'

Rosalind felt her heart beat faster. 'For ever' meant promises.

He released her hands and struggled to take something from his jacket pocket.

She felt as if she was melting inside when she saw it was a ring box. He looked up at her, but she could say nothing, breathless again.

Carefully, he opened the box. Standing up on its velvet cushion, the ring was dominated by a solitaire emerald which glittered in the reflection from the table lamp.

He took the ring from the box and with his other hand took one of Rosalind's.

'Rosalind, will you make me the happiest man in the world — will you be my wife?'

She thought she'd never get the words out, for her throat was tight with emotion.

'Oh, yes, Nicol,' she finally managed to breathe.

He slipped the ring on her third finger and then kissed her hand.

'I chose the stone especially to match your beautiful eyes.'

'I'm so happy,' she said, but it came out all wavery as tears filled her eyes.

Afterwards, Rosalind couldn't have said what she ate, she just remembered it as the meal of a lifetime, all suffused with laughter and joy. Somewhere in the background there was a vague chatter of voices, a muted clatter of cutlery, but only Nicol existed for her.

The waitress finally brought them coffee.

'I hope our wedding can be soon . . . ' Nicol said.

'Me, too, but let me get used to being

engaged first.' She grinned at him. She didn't say, but she wondered about a Christmas wedding. By then the theatre would surely be on its feet and she might not be so much involved in the running of things. Anyway, she'd have Nicol to help her over the next few months.

'You see, they want me back in Canada as soon as I can arrange it,' he said.

'You have to go away again?' She was disappointed.

'More than that, my love. The construction company has given me a permanent position — chief engineer! The job I've always wanted. And you will just love Canada, Rosalind. A country of such beauty and space and opportunity.' He beamed at her. 'I can't wait to take you back with me to start our new life there.'

★   ★   ★

Gil stood by the office window, watching Nicol and Rosalind cross the street, running down by the side of the theatre. As they stepped off the pavement, Nicol took Rosalind's hand and she turned and gave him a stunning smile. Their heads almost touched. They were a handsome couple.

Well, Nicol had been a bolt from the blue. Gil had had no idea that Rosalind had a boyfriend, let alone one who was so close to her. Mind you, her private life was her own and there was no reason why she should have mentioned him before, yet Gil felt a sense of unease.

He could hardly fault Nicol, though. Once the introductions were over, he'd shown a keen interest in the theatre and in everyone who worked there. Gil had noticed that he asked sensible and pertinent questions about any problems they might have found with the structure of the building and other related aspects. That was his job, of course, construction.

Perhaps Gil was just being selfish, but he had thought all Rosalind's energies were focused on the Limelight as well as her office job. Would the reappearance of Nicol affect her work here? The despair he'd felt at the thought of losing the theatre before the Forsyth girls had appeared had all but dissipated when Rosalind and Beatrice had thrown themselves into supporting it.

But he must keep thinking positively and he wanted to talk to Beatrice, too.

Gil found her backstage and asked her to come back to the office with him.

'You don't mind me being here for the show tonight?' she asked in her direct way as soon as she followed him into the room. 'I rather got the impression that Nicol and Rosalind wanted to be alone.' She lowered the register of her voice on the last word, making it sound romantic and dramatic.

Gil laughed.

'Well spotted. Actually, I wanted to have a chat with you.'

Beatrice perched on the edge of his desk.

'Shoot, man,' she said in her best American gangster's moll impression.

'Your performance in 'HMS Pinafore' was first class,' Gil declared.

She almost slid off the desk. Her blue eyes were wide with apprehension.

'You were there? How did you know about it?' she whispered. 'It was meant to be a secret.'

Gil held up his hand in a gesture of peace.

'It was a slip of the tongue on Stuart's part. But why did you want it kept secret?'

'Rosalind didn't want you to think I'd try to use my experience to ask for parts here,' she said honestly.

'But that's just what I do want!'

Beatrice's mouth fell open.

Gil sat back in his chair.

'I think you've got great potential, and I could offer you work here. OK, it's the lowest rung of the ladder — assistant stage manager, which means doing all kinds of jobs backstage while you learn stagecraft.'

'I know what an ASM does.' Beatrice nodded enthusiastically.

'Then maybe you know, too, that an ASM can take small acting parts to begin with?'

Her eyes lit up.

'But . . . I mean, do you think I'm good enough to be taken on?'

Gil shrugged.

'I wouldn't be sitting here offering you the job if I didn't think you were.'

'Oh, Gil, this would be my greatest dream come true.' She gave a great gust of a sigh, then gradually the euphoric expression disappeared and was replaced by a tiny frown.

'Is there a problem, Beatrice?'

'It's just that Rosalind wants me to go to drama college,' she said forlornly.

'Fair enough point,' he said. 'But here you'll be living the theatre, day in, day out, finding out how it operates on every level. Another important point is that by acting now, you'll qualify much faster for your Equity card.'

'The last point of consideration,

though, is that you'll not be paid much, but enough to keep you fed, at least.'

There was a momentary pause, then her face lit up again and she gave him one of her hundred-watt smiles.

'That's all I need to know! I'd like to take the job.' She held out her hand to him.

He wondered at the sudden change, although he shook her hand to seal the deal.

'What about Rosalind?' he asked.

'Oh, she'll see the benefit,' she said airily. 'She won't have to pay college fees.'

Well, it was a point, Gil conceded to himself, but he had a sneaking suspicion that he should make this right with Rosalind next time he saw her.

'Anyway, nothing lost if you help out tonight,' he said briskly. 'Let's go backstage and start work.'

He watched as she danced out the door and made for the stairs. Her fair beauty would certainly catch the eye on stage. She had a lot of talent, but her training would require a firm hand.

Although she wouldn't have breathed a word of it to anyone, Livvy was bored stiff. The days of her pregnancy seemed to be dragging now. She felt one hundred per cent fit, but if she knitted or crocheted one more garment, their child would have a new outfit for almost every day of the year.

Donald took great care of her, of course, but she was feeling a bit left out — of the theatre, that was. Even Donald had linked up with his coach tour stop-offs at the Limelight.

She had puzzled over what she could do to help in any way and had come up with the idea of writing a history of the Limelight. It would hardly be strenuous work, doing the research from old theatre programmes and newspaper reviews. Besides, she could interview some of the older members of the company.

For now, however, she had to keep

her plans to herself. There was something far more important on the cards tonight. She was hosting an engagement party for Rosalind and Nicol.

'There's enough food here to cater for Jardine's, the theatre and our bus company,' Donald remarked as he carried trays from the kitchen to the dining room. 'And it's only a family party.'

'I could have asked more folk but I didn't have much time,' she said.

'You mean the engagement is a bit out of the blue,' he replied.

'Oh, well, certainly we didn't expect it so soon, but absence makes the heart grow fonder and all that.' Livvy re-arranged a plate of savouries.

★ ★ ★

Later, Livvy had to admit that Rosalind looked almost transformed. She was wearing a dress of deep green chiffon, which emphasised her slim shape and also highlighted her magnificent engagement ring. Her eyes shone with happiness and her whole bearing was one of some-one who was confident with her life.

Livvy had almost forgotten how handsome Nicol was. Tonight, resplen-dent in his kilt, his height seemed more arresting, his face permanently wreathed in smiles. She noticed, too, how easy he was in company, interested in everyone and paying attention to what they said, even her tales of domesticity!

It wasn't long, however, before he got on to the subject of Canada.

'It's not so far away,' he told them as they sat round the dining-table, finish-ing off a bottle of champagne. 'You'll all be able to visit and we'll be back to check up on you all, as often as we can.'

Rosalind had mentioned Canada to Livvy on the phone but it was quite different facing the reality that her sister was going to be living so far away. Livvy felt quite bereft but tried to hide it at this special time.

'Whatever you do, make the wedding some time after September,' Livvy pleaded. 'Otherwise, I won't be able to find an outfit!'

'I wouldn't dream of going before the arrival of my niece of nephew,' Rosalind assured her with a quick squeeze of her hand.

Livvy didn't miss the quick look Nicol sent her sister. Surely he hadn't planned on going back before then!

'Tell us about the new job, then?' Donald now asked him.

Livvy half-heard Nicol explaining the details of the construction job but didn't miss the hint that he was expected to start work within a few weeks.

'As soon as that?' Donald was surprised. 'Not giving you much time to organise things.'

Nicol smiled at Rosalind.

'We don't plan a long engagement — there's so much of our life out there just waiting for us.'

Rosalind grasped his outstretched hand. Livvy was glad she'd kept her selfish thoughts to herself. Rosalind deserved this happiness.

'And what about the theatre, Rosalind?' Donald asked in his direct, bluff way.

Livvy longed to kick him under the table. That was not quite tactful at the moment.

'I reckon it's on the right lines now.' Rosalind beamed. 'Gil's been marvellous and once I get someone to handle the accounts side, he'll be able to run it easily.'

'And anyway,' Beatrice chipped in, 'he'll have me to help him.'

'Oh, yes,' Livvy teased softly. 'And just how will that work?'

'*Work* is the word.' Beatrice beamed at everyone. 'Now, for my big surprise. I've got a job at the Limelight!'

Silence seemed suspended in the air for a moment or two, then Rosalind leaned forward in her chair.

'A job? Doing what?' she asked.

'Gil's taken me on as ASM,' Beatrice declared.

'When did this happen?' Rosalind

asked, a tiny frown crossing her face.

'He offered it to me on Saturday. I didn't say anything to you, because of your engagement which is much more important.' Beatrice smiled tentatively at Rosalind. 'And guess what? Avril Beaton is going to give me voice training — it's something she teaches in her spare time.'

Livvy passed round more food. She knew her sisters very well and was aware of tension in the air.

'I thought you were going to drama college?' Donald then asked, not helping matters.

'Well, that was the plan, but Gil said I'd learn as much at the theatre — and faster. And . . . ' She turned and shot a smile at Rosalind. 'He's going to pay me a wage, so we'll save on fees.'

Livvy watched the play of expressions on Rosalind's face. She was much too happy at present to make a fuss, but Livvy knew the signs. Her sister was annoyed at this development, taken without even consulting her.

It was something of a habit ingrained in Rosalind — to feel she was responsible for her younger sisters — but perhaps the time had come when she had to let Beatrice find her own feet.

And given Rosalind's own circumstances, what could she do? If she was going away, surely Beatrice would be much happier at the theatre?

Livvy signalled to Donald to fetch more wine. This was a celebration and she was determined to keep that to the forefront. Yet she guessed she was not the only one in the room wondering just what the future did hold for the Forsyth girls.

★ ★ ★

Andrew Jardine was a creature of habit and liked to observe little private rituals. On Monday mornings, he never took the lift up to his office on the third floor, but instead took the grand staircase to the first floor and then up from each gallery to the top. He endeavoured to have a chat with as many of his staff as possible on his perambulation.

This morning, however, his thoughts kept flying to the most unusual weekend he'd spent in a long time. Passing the beauty counter, he gave Beatrice a friendly nod, mainly to remind her he hadn't forgotten that she'd tendered her resignation from Jardine's to work at the Limelight.

Highly unorthodox, but he could understand her enthusiasm for joining the theatre staff. The actress, Avril Beaton, had cheered her on all the way and even offered to coach her with singing.

As he passed through 'Ladies' Gowns' he hoped Avril would take up his invitation to attend the next Mannequin Parade and perhaps choose some outfits. She could become a valued customer and enhance the reputation of Jardine House.

But by far the most surprising event of the weekend had been the arrival of

Nicol Mitchell. Andrew knew that Rosalind had a male friend somewhere in the background but was astounded at the revelation that their friendship was, well, so intimate. He didn't approve of public displays of emotion, but after meeting Nicol he put it all down to sheer impulsiveness.

Yet, though he was fond of Rosalind himself, he couldn't help admitting that she had made a good choice. There was absolutely no side to Nicol. He appeared to be an easy-going chap, yet paid acute attention to detail, and Andrew had been surprised just how much he knew about his own retail business. And gratified that he had admired the unique interior structure of Jardine House.

But now that he had a clue the way the wind was blowing, he wanted to make sure of something vital to him.

As ever, Rosalind arrived early and Andrew wasted no time in asking her to join him in his office.

'What a great weekend I had,' he told

her right away. 'Your theatre is fascinating and you have a wonderful company there.'

Rosalind smiled and murmured something about his enjoying the show.

'Something of a novelty for me but Miss Beaton was kind enough to educate me a little in the progress of the drama,' he said.

Again she smiled, rather demurely, Andrew thought.

'Now,' he said after a pause. 'It made me see how hard you are working and I want to show my appreciation by giving you a raise in wages.'

At that Rosalind's head came up.

'I'm not unaware of how much extra effort and time you put into your job here and I think you should be properly compensated.' Andrew knew he was sounding a little pompous but he didn't want to say what he was actually feeling — that this romance with Nicol might persuade her to leave Jardine House.

Rosalind stared at him for a moment.

'Thank you, Andrew, I appreciate that. I haven't forgotten my earlier mistake and can assure you that my mind is entirely focused on Jardine House during my working hours here. However, there is a 'but' . . . '

It wasn't quite the response Andrew had expected but he felt he had secured Rosalind's services for the future.

'No buts, Rosalind, you deserve this raise.' He moved a few papers about his desk then smiled benignly at her again. 'I like Nicol. It goes without saying he has good taste.' He smiled at her. 'He seems an ideal companion for you, Rosalind.'

'Yes,' she said and then, after a brief hesitation, continued. 'I'm going to marry him, Andrew — that accounts for the 'but'. You might not want to offer me the raise, although I do feel it has been earned . . . ' She gave him a mischievous grin.

'Marry him?' Andrew had only heard the first part of her answer.

'He asked me on Saturday and I

accepted.' She held out her left hand and he saw the emerald ring winking on her finger.

'Oh, I see,' he said, trying to hide his shock. 'I, er, presume you will have a long engagement like most couples.'

To his surprise he saw the briefest of frowns flit across her face.

'No date has been arranged for the wedding.' She bit her lip. 'But we will be settling in Canada as Nicol has been offered a job there.'

He was shaken. Canada, indeed! He twirled a pen between his fingers. At last he managed to say the right thing.

'Congratulations. I hope you'll be very happy.' He tried to sound enthusiastic.

'Thank you.' She stood up, not knowing what else to say. 'Now, I must get those figures all present and correct for you. Thank you for the raise.'

She left his office and Andrew flung the pen across his desk.

★ ★ ★

Rain pelted down on Friday evening as Rosalind alighted from the tram in Byres Road and climbed up Great George Street. She was carrying two heavy message bags to boot and hoped the contents wouldn't be soggy by the time she reached the flat.

Indoors, she stripped off her coat, put it over a clothes-horse and stuffed newspapers into her damp shoes. Next she laid the groceries on the kitchen table and began to prepare the evening meal.

This had been the most wonderful week. She'd had no idea how wonderful it was to feel cherished. Nicol had filled all their time together with love and fun. She felt as if she was existing in a circle of warmth.

He was different from the Nicol who had left Scotland weeks ago. He'd returned with a new confidence, coupled with a sense of determination. She guessed it was all to do with the success of his contract and was glad for him. He'd struggled to find his niche in the world since leaving the RAF.

Beatrice had asked Stuart along for a meal tonight, and with Nicol present, too, it would be a happy foursome. At least, she hoped so. Rosalind wasn't sure how Stuart had reacted to the news that Beatrice was leaving tomorrow for Lockhart.

Rosalind sliced an onion with quick, sharp cuts. How could Gil have given her sister a job without even mentioning it to her? Well, she'd have to deal with it tactfully while making sure Gil knew she should have been consulted. She didn't want to upset him too much as he didn't yet know about her engagement to Nicol, let alone their plans to move to Canada.

All week she had been resisting Nicol's request to name a wedding date. She was determined not to leave Scotland before Livvy's baby arrived. Her sister had such an open, guileless face that Rosalind hadn't missed the bereft expression when Livvy realised that Canada was a reality.

Stuart was a bit moody when he arrived but to Rosalind's relief the meal went very well, due in great part to Nicol, who employed his sense of humour to deflect any potential arguments.

'My one appearance on the stage was in a school play,' he told them. 'Believe it or not, I was a very earnest child and learned the whole play — all the parts. The result was that I shouted out every cue if there was the slightest hesitation on the part of a fellow actor.'

'That couldn't have made you very popular.' Stuart laughed.

'Not with my fellow thespians,' Nicol agreed. 'And even worse with my teachers. A serious drama turned into a riotous comedy as the audience were in stitches every time I opened my mouth.'

Their laughter was almost drowned out by a deafening clap of thunder.

Beatrice jumped up to switch on the lights as night seemed to have fallen without warning.

'Just look at those clouds,' she said.

Outside, roll upon roll of ominous black clouds were unfurling across the roofs of the city.

'I hope it's better tomorrow,' Nicol said. 'I'm going to the seaside . . . '

★ ★ ★

Donald had offered to take both girls, together with Beatrice's luggage, on the coach to Lockhart. Nicol and Stuart had asked to join them and now they were all ready to embark on the trip.

'Glad to see the rain has stopped at last,' Livvy said as she waited to see them off. 'It was some night — I hardly slept.'

The sky was now a pale blue as if the storm had rinsed it thoroughly.

Soon they set off for Ayrshire. Donald's passengers were on a full day trip, going as far as Burns' Cottage at Ayr, then back up to Lockhart and the evening performance at the Limelight.

After a stop in Largs for morning

coffee, the coach set off again. Beatrice had chatted almost non-stop to Stuart.

'Will she be able to keep to a script?' Nicol whispered in Rosalind's ear.

'Oh, yes, I reckon that underneath all the chatter is a dedicated actress just waiting to get out. All her amateur performances have been beautifully judged. Just don't tell her I said that,' Rosalind confided.

Would Gil really be able to give her the necessary training, she wondered. It would be a tragedy if Beatrice didn't make it on to the professional stage.

Donald finally stopped the coach in the square on the opposite side from the theatre.

'There it is, folks, the theatre where we'll finish our day's trip,' he said to his passengers. Everyone strained to see but few made any comment.

Rosalind could understand that. The theatre looked rather deserted, with no lights showing at all at this time of day. The stonework looked dull, probably a leftover from the previous evening's rain. Still, it would be sparkling like a glittery star when the party returned for the show.

Nicol and Stuart lugged Beatrice's suitcases across the square. As they approached, Gil suddenly appeared at the main entrance.

Rosalind noticed at once his grim expression. For a moment she thought he'd heard about her engagement and wasn't pleased. Then she realised he wouldn't be that petty.

'Is something wrong?' she asked Gil when they reached the theatre.

'The storm last night . . . ' he began.

'Yes, we had it in Glasgow, too,' she said.

'Come in through the foyer,' he said, as if she hadn't spoken, and led the way into the theatre.

Inside it was dark, not a light in the place. Had the storm knocked out the electricity? Then, as they moved into the auditorium, Rosalind was conscious of a pervading smell which she couldn't instantly identify.

Behind her, she heard Nicol and Stuart dump the suitcases, murmuring to each other. At that moment Gil stopped in his tracks and indicated that she and Beatrice should go first.

Instinct told her that something dreadful was wrong and she felt a tremble of anxiety course through her body. As she walked down the centre aisle she became aware of a source of light, but it wasn't electrical.

'Rosalind?' Beatrice's low, uncertain tone indicated that she, too, was uneasy.

Beatrice waited for her sister and reached for her hand.

As they approached the stage, Rosalind's eyes discerned some kind of chaos in the orchestra pit. Closer still, she saw smashed music stands, the grand piano listing to one side and, everywhere in the pit, heaps of rubble.

At the same time, her brain identified the sounds beneath their feet. Squelching. The carpet was sodden. She also realised that it was natural light beaming straight down into the orchestra pit.

'Look up,' Gil said in her ear.

Jerkily, Rosalind tipped back her head.

There was a great gaping hole in the roof, showing a now innocent blue sky above. Around the jagged edges of the hole, water was dripping like intermittent rain on to the stage, carpet, the stall seats, and the five of them. She heard Nicol give a low whistle of horror.

'This is awful!' Stuart murmured.

There was a sob from Beatrice.

'Oh, not our lovely theatre!'

Rosalind didn't need Gil to tell her that the storm had wrought colossal damage. She couldn't tell, though, if the roof was beyond repair.

Had they fought all the other problems so far only to be defeated by nature? Rosalind's shoulders sagged. She could not walk away from this, but could this be the end of the dream for Gil, the company and Beatrice?

5

For a moment, time was suspended. The dampness and lack of light emphasised the leaden atmosphere. Rosalind was aware of several members of the company, including Polly and Jock, standing silent on the stage, looking despondent. She guessed they were expecting her to deal with the situation.

'Right.' Rosalind squared her shoulders and forced a positive tone into her voice. 'First of all, let's see what we can do about this mess.'

'I contacted a local roofer to come in and make a temporary repair,' Gil told her, filling a wheelbarrow with debris.

'Thanks, Gil, that was quick thinking.' She sketched a grateful smile and their eyes met. She saw in his expression the same quiet determination that she felt and a faint hope stirred in her. She wasn't alone in taking this on her shoulders after all. They were in this together.

'Of course, we can't get a proper repair under way until the insurance people have assessed the damage,' he went on.

'I expect they'll have to approve the cost,' Rosalind said automatically, but a chill of unease had gripped her. She had seen the insurance documents, but couldn't remember the exact terms.

She felt Nicol's arm slide around her shoulder.

'Rosalind, my love, you have to be sensible about this. The roof could be beyond repair. This is an old theatre — there could be other structural damage,' he said.

'Well, we might have to face that possibility,' she replied evenly. 'But for the moment we have to carry on. We haven't come this far with the Limelight to give up now!'

She saw the tenseness in Gil's shoulders relax a little and again their eyes met. Despite the ups and downs they'd encountered so far, they thought and cared for the theatre in the same way.

There was a subdued cheer from the stage area and she looked up to give everyone an encouraging smile.

'When is the roofer coming?' she asked Gil.

'Any time now,' he said.

'In that case, we'd better get started and clear up this mess,' Polly announced and clambered down from the stage.

'Now, I reckon we need shovels and some good muscle,' Jock said, following her down into the stalls.

Rosalind's heart warmed when she saw everyone immediately spring to help. Someone was despatched to find the tools, and others began man-handling smaller bits of rubble.

'Dump everything on the stage in the meantime. We can dispose of it outside later,' Gil said to the helpers, then turned to Rosalind. 'I've cancelled the bookings for the next three weeks. I reckon it will take that time to get the roof sorted out.'

'Gil, are you being practical?' Nicol sounded worried. 'This could take much longer to repair.'

'We can't afford to be closed for several weeks,' Gil replied, then turned to Rosalind. 'I spoke on the phone to Avril earlier. She's a real trouper. Took her cancellation on the chin and promised to be first back with a free show when we're in business again.'

Rosalind nodded.

'Oh, my goodness, I'd forgotten about Donald! We have to tell him that tonight's show is cancelled. He's taken his passengers to the Urquhart Arms Hotel for lunch. Beatrice, will you go and give him the bad news?'

'On our way.' Beatrice signalled Stuart to follow her and they made their way out of the theatre.

'Will you have to compensate Donald for the cancelled booking?' Nicol asked.

'Yes, of course,' Rosalind said positively, while trying to keep the worry from her tone. She hadn't thought of that and probably they'd have to pay the touring companies whose shows Gil had cancelled. She had no idea how much all that would cost.

'Maybe we could take a quick look at the insurance cover we have?' she asked Gil. 'Will you stay here and help?' She turned to Nicol. 'I think another pair of strong arms would be much appreciated.'

Nicol looked annoyed, but he began to help loading the wheelbarrow with rubble. She needed to discuss the business with Gil alone. Much as she loved Nicol, she knew he didn't share her feelings or indeed completely understand her commitment towards the theatre.

His mind was entirely focused on their impending marriage and departure for Canada. That was her wish, too, but she had not only to think of Beatrice, but also the whole company. For the moment she had to concentrate on that and not be distracted by her personal affairs.

* ★ ★

Once in the theatre office, Gil took the insurance files from the cabinet.

'Keith Wilson handled all this,' he said, 'but I'm sure he was careful about the cover.'

Together they read through the document. Rosalind turned over a page.

'It looks like Keith might have left us disastrously underinsured,' she lamented. 'We might have to find half the money ourselves!'

'You're joking!' Gil grimly scanned the document. 'Why on earth did Keith let that slip?'

'He was probably doing his best to keep the theatre going,' she said, trying to be fair. 'Cutting down on that aspect of insurance probably saved a bit of money, and he could never have anticipated anything like this damage.'

'I don't understand all the small print in this.' Gil was frowning at the document. 'I can't work out exactly what sum the theatre is insured for and if it is going to be enough to pay for repairs.'

'Nor can I,' she said. 'I wonder if Andrew Jardine would look over this for us? He will know all about buildings insurance.'

'Good idea. Could you take it to his office on Monday?'

She nodded her agreement.

They were summoned back to the auditorium when Jock came to tell them that the roofer had arrived.

Rosalind was introduced to Bert Saunders, a local man clearly well known to Gil.

'That's not a pretty sight,' Bert said, leaning backwards and assessing the hole in the roof.

'Can you make the theatre watertight for the present?' Rosalind asked him.

'That's my job, lass,' he said, smiling.

Rosalind had to be content with that. He was clearly a man of few words but she understood his professional approach.

'OK, gang,' Gil said. 'Since we can do nothing more at the moment I suggest you all go home and have some rest. You've all been real troupers.'

The company dispersed, promising to come back later in the day.

Nicol offered to go out and get some sandwiches for himself, Rosalind and Gil as they didn't want to leave the theatre. They sat and ate the scrap meal and drank the pot of tea Gil had rustled up. Conversation was minimal. They were all too occupied with their thoughts and worries.

Eventually Bert Saunders knocked on the office door.

'All shipshape for now,' he said. 'The roof will hold good until it's properly repaired, provided we don't get a repeat storm. Your chandeliers are OK and there's no damage to any electrical fittings.'

'How bad is the roof?' Gil asked him.

'It's going to cost a pretty penny to make it secure again.' Bert was frank.

'How much do you estimate?' Rosalind asked him.

He quoted a sum which Rosalind knew left Gil reeling as much as she, although they both covered it by merely raising their eyebrows.

'I can do the work for you, but you'll have to get approval from your insurance company,' Bert told them.

'That seems a staggering amount to me,' Nicol said when Bert had left.

'I suppose it is.' Gil was noncommittal.

Rosalind didn't need him to spell it out. Somehow, instinctively, they suspected that the insurance premiums would be stretched to cover that amount and that was only if the insurers agreed to the repair.

Otherwise, they would have to find the money themselves. On top of that there was the compensation to the touring companies and, more importantly, the wages of the company while the theatre was out of action.

She felt sick with despair. They couldn't rely on local support for a second time so how on earth were they ever going to be able to pay for everything?

* * *

Once outside the theatre, Stuart asked Beatrice to stop for a moment.

'I've got something important to tell you,' he said.

'Later, Stuart, let's get this over with first.' She hurried on.

Inside the hotel, Beatrice asked Donald to join them at a corner table, away from his passengers. When they told him what had happened he stared at them with utter disbelief.

'It's just awful, Donald.' Tears ran down Beatrice's cheeks. 'There's this great hole in the roof and rubble everywhere and the seats and carpets are all soaking.'

'So what are you going to do?' Donald was still numb with shock.

'Well, tonight is off for a start,' Stuart said.

'Oh, no — my first trip and this has

to happen,' Donald said angrily.

'We didn't cause the storm.' Beatrice recovered enough to point out that it was hardly the theatre's fault. 'Please apologise to your passengers on our behalf, Donald.'

'They've been done out of their show,' Donald said doggedly.

★　★　★

It dawned on Stuart that Donald hadn't realised just how devastating the damage was.

'Maybe you could try to get seats for them somewhere else,' Stuart suggested. 'Why not try the Ayr Gaiety? You're going down that way after lunch, aren't you?'

'Aye, that's true.' Donald stood up from the table and prepared to rejoin his passengers. 'I had my doubts about the Limelight from the very beginning . . . '

'Oh, Donald, it's just a temporary problem. And we will reimburse you for tonight,' Beatrice assured him.

'Fine,' Donald said and walked away.

'Can you reimburse him for tonight?' Stuart asked Beatrice as they left the hotel.

'I've no idea, but I had to make the offer,' she said. 'Come on, let's go back and help with the clearing up.'

Stuart caught her hand.

'Bea, why don't you have second thoughts about taking this job here? To be frank, I don't think the Limelight is going to survive this and you'll be out of work, having given up your post at Jardine House.'

'Don't be such a pessimist.' She pulled her hand away. 'Of course the theatre is going to survive.' She began to walk back to the hotel entrance.

'You don't know that,' he persisted. 'You don't know anything about running it. You've just said you've no idea if Donald can be reimbursed.'

'I leave all that to Rosalind. She has the mathematical brain. I'm just an actress.' She stopped and faced him.

'And nothing, I mean nothing, is going to stop me being one!'

As they left the hotel, they noticed Polly approaching from the other side of the road.

'The roofer has arrived and we're all in the way.' She took Beatrice's arm. 'Let's go round to my place and you can see your room. It's only two doors up.'

Stuart held back. This was the woman who was giving Beatrice lodgings in Lockhart. Did she really think the theatre could be saved, too, or was she living in the same dream-world as Beatrice?

'Good to meet you at last.' Polly shook his hand. 'Budding scriptwriter, aren't you?'

He was surprised and darted a glance at Beatrice.

'Oh, I know all about you, young man. Beatrice here is very proud of you.' Polly paused and gave him an assessing look. 'As, I am sure, you are of her.'

Stuart hesitated for a moment.

'Yes, of course.'

'I should think so,' Polly replied, searching in her handbag for her house key.

A few moments later, she opened the front door of her house.

'Your room is upstairs, Beatrice, second door on the right. Have a look while I get us something to eat.' She turned to Stuart. 'Come into the kitchen, Stuart, while she's upstairs.'

The kitchen was as bright and colourful as Polly herself. She indicated that he should take a chair while she briskly filled a kettle.

'You've got to let her do this,' she said.

He stared at her.

'It's written all over you that you're against her moving to Lockhart,' she went on. 'You have a very open face.'

'I'm not against her acting, but she's rushed into this without much thought. And look what's happened today — it could be the end of the theatre!

157

Besides, she had a nice little job in Jardine House and did plenty of acting in her spare time.' He sent a challenging look to Polly.

'That was never going to be enough for her.' Polly sat down opposite him. 'Quite rightly so. She's a very talented girl and willing to work hard at any task in the theatre.'

'Don't write off the Limelight yet, Stuart. And, believe me, if she doesn't act here she'll find another theatre to take her on.' She stood up and set out some cups and saucers.

'I know you're upset that she's here and you're stuck in Glasgow all week, she told me all that,' she went on. 'That doesn't mean she doesn't care for you!'

'I'm not sure about that,' he replied.

'Let me tell you this, young man. That girl's heart is in the right place and she cares for you. You have to show you care for her. If you make her leave Lockhart, then you'll lose her. Is that what you want?'

Stuart stared at Polly. He wanted

Beatrice back in Glasgow with him, especially now that he had to remain there himself. He'd been waiting until they were alone to give her his news.

Torry Dunbar, the young comedian who had starred in the same show as Avril Beaton at the Grand Duchess, had accepted one of his scripts and wanted Stuart to work on more with him, but it had to be in Glasgow. Stuart realised this was his opportunity to break into the theatre or radio.

Now it seemed he had no alternative but to leave Beatrice here, with a precarious job situation and without him. The prospect was heart-breaking.

★ ★ ★

Avril Beaton swanned through the entrance of Jardine House, regally nodding at the liveried doorman as he greeted her.

'I've come to see Mr Jardine. I'm a personal friend,' she told him.

'Fourth floor, madam. Allow me to

escort you to the elevator.'

Avril gave him one of her show-stopping smiles. She was rather tickled to be back in Jardine House, this time as a successful and well-known actress in Glasgow. Many was the time she'd sashayed through the departments as a teenager on Saturday mornings, pretending to be someone important and enjoying the theatricality of it all.

She was directed to Andrew's office and knocked on the door.

'Come,' she heard from within.

Andrew was sitting at his desk, head bowed over papers. It was a few seconds before he looked up.

Then he jumped to his feet, a faint flush lighting up his face.

'Avril! Oh, I'm so sorry, I thought it was one of my staff. How lovely to see you! Please sit down.'

Avril was delighted with the warmth of his welcome.

'Please — what will you have, tea or coffee and some of our famous cakes?' he asked.

'Coffee only, please, Andrew.' She took off her gloves and put them on the edge of his desk.

He lifted his telephone and dialled. It was answered immediately and he ordered coffee to be sent up.

'Now . . . ' He smiled at her, rather shyly, she thought. 'To what do I owe this pleasure?'

'I'm really pleased to see you, but I have bad news and also a favour to ask you,' she said, her tone serious. In a few short sentences she gave him the gist of Gil's phone call to her that morning.

'Oh, no, poor Rosalind, she has worked so hard to get the theatre up and running.' He tapped his fingers together for a moment, frowning. 'I take it that the roof can be repaired?'

'A temporary repair is being made today to keep any further rain out,' Avril said, a little dismayed that Andrew's first reaction had been to think of Rosalind. 'Actually, my favour was in the nature of visiting the theatre tomorrow. I want to give Gil and

161

everyone my support and I was sure you would feel the same way.'

'Of course,' Andrew agreed at once. 'We can drive down in the morning if that suits you?'

'Thank you, that would be ideal,' she replied.

The coffee arrived then and it gave her time to phrase delicately her next question to him.

'You're very fond of Rosalind, I can tell,' she said.

Andrew leaned back in his chair.

'I've always had a bit of a soft spot for her, mainly because she's been a godsend to Jardine House in her capacity here. She has an astute brain and it's typical of her to take up the challenge of the Limelight when, frankly, it's quite outside her experience.'

Avril stirred her coffee.

'Are you upset by her engagement to Nicol?' she asked in a casual manner.

He gave a rueful laugh.

'Only in that I will lose one of my

best employees, but I can't let Jardine House stand in the way of her happiness.'

Avril took a sip. She had the answer she wanted. Fond as he might be of Rosalind, Andrew had no romantic notions in that direction.

'I wonder if there's anything I can do to help them in Lockhart?' he mused. 'I know better than to offer Rosalind money; she's too proud for that. Tell you what, once I've assessed the damage maybe I can help out with furnishings and fabrics from the store?'

Avril smiled. He was a thoroughly nice man. She was so glad they'd met and that they had this link with the theatre. She picked up her gloves, preparing to leave, when he took her by surprise.

'Since you have no show tonight, Avril, perhaps you are free for dinner . . . ?'

★ ★ ★

'That settles it,' Livvy said, when Donald gave her the news on his return from Ayrshire that evening. 'Everyone keeps telling me that there's no need for me to go to Lockhart, but now I've decided. I want to be with my sisters and give them moral support.'

'That's madness, Livvy,' Donald protested. 'Not in your condition.'

'Why does everybody go on about my condition?' she retorted. 'It's perfectly normal to have a baby. And believe me, I worry more just sitting here doing nothing than I would if I could see exactly what is going on at the Limelight. I want to be involved, Donald. After all, I do own one-third of the theatre.'

'That's not going to amount to much if there's a whopping great bill to pay for repairs,' he pointed out.

'Maybe so, but I'd like to show my support, particularly to Rosalind. She should be thinking about her wedding first and foremost, not this crisis. Somehow I think Beatrice will be focused more on performing on the stage.' She sent her husband a pleading look. 'Please, Donald, can we go to Lockhart tomorrow, even for just an hour? It isn't as if you have any bookings.'

Donald sighed.

'Well, if it will put your mind at rest. No more than an hour, then.'

* * *

By the time they arrived next day, Livvy was surprised to find so many people buzzing around.

'We stayed overnight,' Rosalind explained, 'so that we could do some more clearing up first thing today. We've managed to lift all the soaked carpets and the upholstery from the seating.'

'Rosalind, you were so right when you said it is a lovely little theatre.' Livvy gazed round the auditorium.

'You should have seen it yesterday,' Beatrice chimed in. 'Water everywhere, the hole in the roof and all the rubble.

The main thing is that it's going to be repaired and will be back to normal soon.'

Livvy did not miss the frown on Rosalind's face, nor the quick glance she sent to Gil. She drew her sister aside.

'I can't do much for you at present, only offer moral support,' she said.

'Just to have you here is great, Livvy.' Rosalind gave her a quick hug. 'We can do nothing more until the insurance surveyor has a look at the damage.'

'Who's that?' Livvy whispered to her as two figures came down the aisle.

'Oh, it's Andrew Jardine, my boss and — '

'My goodness, the lady is the actress Avril Beaton! We saw her at that theatre in Glasgow.' Livvy sounded thrilled.

Andrew Jardine shook Livvy's hand formally, but Avril Beaton was much more relaxed.

'Aha, you are the mysterious third owner of the theatre! How nice to meet you.' She held Livvy at arm's length.

'You look so well, my dear. How long before the happy event?'

'About a couple of months.' Livvy smiled at her, completely taken by her friendly manner.

'Donald, would you like to come to the office and we can settle up?' Gil asked.

'And Andrew, could we ask you to look over our insurance policy?' Rosalind asked him.

'In that case, perhaps I could show you over the theatre, Livvy. I understand you haven't visited since you were a little girl?' Avril said.

'Oh, I'd love that. We never did get to see backstage or anything. All I know is what Rosalind and Beatrice have told me.' Livvy was delighted.

'Now, take care, Livvy, and don't tire yourself,' Donald instructed as he left with Gil to go to the office.

'He's such a fusspot,' Livvy whispered to Avril as the actress led her backstage.

'Why not?' Avril replied with a laugh.

'Caring men are very special. See you later, Andrew,' she called as he went off to join the others in the office.

★ ★ ★

Gil could see that Donald was reluctant to take a cheque to cover his losses.

'No, we insist, Donald. No-one else should go short on account of our misfortune. You have a business to run, too.'

'With a bit of luck they might be able to claim it all on the insurance,' Nicol chimed in.

The three men looked over to the desk where Andrew and Rosalind were poring over the insurance documents.

'I'll take it with me,' Andrew said to Rosalind. 'It needs a professional eye to define the terms.'

There was something in his tone that set off alarm bells in Gil's head. He moved over to the desk.

'The premiums don't seem very high, so perhaps the total of insurance isn't high, either.'

Andrew was folding up the documents and putting them inside his pocket.

'Not at first glance.' The look Andrew gave Gil was honest. 'There seem to have been several adjustments over the years and it needs someone to work out exactly where you stand.'

'Thanks for this, Andrew,' Gil said gratefully. 'I'm hoping to get an estimate for the repairs tomorrow.'

Andrew nodded.

'Phone Rosalind at the office and she can let me know. Meantime, I'll go and see if I can find Avril.'

'I'll come with you,' Donald said. 'Try to keep my wife from overdoing things.'

* * *

As he was leaving the office, Andrew turned to Rosalind. 'I'd like to take everyone out to lunch, the company included. I think you all could do with a break. Could you run over to the

Urquhart Arms Hotel and book tables?'

'Of course, Andrew, what a generous idea.' Rosalind smiled at him, concealing her true feelings.

He was treating her as an employee, exactly as he did at Jardine House, quite overlooking the fact that she was an independent woman here, and moreover, the boss. But she would never hold that against him. He was a generous man.

'It's not looking good for the insurance,' Nicol observed to Gil when they were alone in the office.

'No,' Gil replied. 'Andrew didn't seem too happy with the details in the policy.'

'How on earth are you going to manage on your own, anyway?' Nicol asked.

Gil stared at him.

'On my own? Rosalind and I have shared the management since Keith left. We'll work this out together.'

'But she won't be here.'

'Oh, agreed, she can only come to

Lockhart at weekends,' Gil conceded. 'She's sensible not to give up her job at Jardine House. I think Andrew needs her there anyway.'

'Not for much longer.'

Gil began to feel uneasy. Nicol was getting at something, something he didn't know.

'Why is that?' He decided to be blunt.

'It's not long until she and I go to Canada,' Nicol said.

'You mean that she is going back with you right away?' Gil's voice was sharp.

'Soon as we are married. You do know that I have a permanent position there now?'

Gil dropped his head and began fiddling with the papers on his desk.

'I knew about your marriage, of course, but not that Rosalind was about to abandon the theatre.'

'She wants to be with me, Gil. And she can hardly run the theatre from the other side of the Atlantic.' Nicol went to the door. 'I'll go and meet her at the hotel now.'

Gil sank down into a chair. He needed Rosalind's business expertise to guide them as he was sure they were facing a huge bill for the roof repair plus the cancelled shows.

In his heart he knew he could not run the Limelight on his own. Despite his admiration for Rosalind, he felt a sense of betrayal and a creeping unease that he had lost everything.

★　★　★

It was as Rosalind and Nicol were returning down the aisle of the theatre that they heard the cry.

'That's Livvy!' Rosalind gasped and ran towards the stage.

To her horror she found her sister lying on the floor.

'What happened?' She bent to help her.

'Nothing much. Didn't look where I was going and tripped.' Livvy took hold of Nicol's arm to help her sit up. 'Look, just got a graze on my shin. Oh, dear, there goes another pair of good stockings!'

'Livvy, are you sure you're all right?' Rosalind began to feel her sister's limbs and then put a hand on her forehead.

'For goodness' sake, Rosalind, stop fussing! Of course I'm all right.' Livvy sounded really cross.

'I'll go and find Donald.' Nicol said and disappeared into the wings.

'Don't, Nicol . . . ' Livvy began. But it was too late. He was out of earshot.

'Donald will be so angry with my clumsiness. He didn't want me to come, but honestly, Rosalind, I'm fed up with the cotton-wool treatment. Help me stand up, please.'

Rosalind hooked the leg of a chair with one of her feet and dragged it over towards her, then gently helped Livvy to sit down.

Her sister took a few deep breaths.

'I'm fine now. Mind you, a cup of tea wouldn't go amiss.'

'As soon as Donald comes back, I'll go and make you one,' Rosalind said.

She'd barely uttered the words when Donald stormed on to the stage.

'Livvy! Are you all right?'

'No, Donald. I probably need an industrial size plaster to cover the graze on my shin! Of course I'm fine!' She was still sounding testy.

'What happened?' he demanded, now down on one knee, examining Livvy's grazed shin.

'I bumped into a chair or something,' she muttered.

'There is a cottage hospital in Lockhart, isn't there, Rosalind?' Donald asked.

By now, some of the company had gathered on the stage.

'Yes, up the hill.' Polly stepped forward. 'Why not take her there and get a doctor to check her out?'

'There's no need,' Livvy protested. 'I'd much rather have a cup of tea.'

Rosalind left the stage to fill the kettle. She worked as fast as she could but by the time she returned, Donald was helping Livvy down the steps into the auditorium.

'They're off to the hospital. It will put his mind at rest,' Polly said to Rosalind.

Rosalind followed Livvy down into the auditorium.

'Shall I come with you?' she asked.

'Don't be silly,' Livvy replied. 'This is a complete waste of time. And I still have lots more to see here.'

'She'll be OK.' Polly touched Rosalind's arm. 'It looks like a graze and perhaps a bruise.'

Rosalind nodded. She took a few deep breaths to calm herself and recalled Livvy's testy reactions. She didn't appear to have hurt herself badly and at least the doctor would examine her carefully.

'I think I'll get myself that tea,' she said to Polly, still more than a little concerned about her sister.

★ ★ ★

'So, when were you going to tell me about your emigration?' Gil spoke to Rosalind for the first time since they'd sat down in the hotel restaurant more than an hour ago.

Rosalind, her mind still focused on Livvy whom she had expected to join them before this, turned round and stared at him.

'Emigration?'

'Nicol tells me you're off to Canada for good as soon as you are married,' he replied.

It was only then that she took in the grim expression on his face.

'Yes, that's true,' she said slowly, conscious that Nicol was sitting on her other side. 'But that won't be for some time yet.'

'I got the impression it was within the next few weeks — in fact, probably before the roof was repaired,' Gil said plainly.

Clearly Nicol had spoken out before she'd had time to prepare Gil. It wasn't that Nicol was trying to force her hand, far from it, but he did have a job to go to and it would not create a good impression if he didn't turn up on the starting date.

At the same time she had said to him

that she wanted to be in Scotland when Livvy's baby arrived and that was two months away.

'I'm not walking out on you, Gil,' Rosalind said. 'We won't be marrying for a few months yet. And before I go, I'll make sure everything in the Limelight is restored as good as new, its future assured, plus we'll find someone to assist you with financial management.'

'Sorry, maybe I jumped the gun,' he apologised.

'I should have made my plans clear before . . . ' she began when a waiter stopped by her chair.

'Are you Miss Rosalind Forsyth?'

'Yes.'

'There's been an urgent phone message for you. Can you and your sister get to the hospital as soon as possible?'

Andrew immediately took them in his car and within minutes they were in the hospital.

A nurse said that Mr and Mrs Webster were in a room at the end of the corridor.

'Do you think the baby's here already?' Beatrice whispered.

They knocked on the door and went in. Livvy was lying on the bed, cradled in Donald's arms. They were both crying.

6

Polly Anderson laid out breakfast on the kitchen table. The porridge was keeping warm on the stove; she'd toasted almost a whole loaf and the teapot was quietly steaming.

Rosalind was the first to come downstairs.

'Oh, there you are.' Polly smiled gently, secretly distressed by Rosalind's drawn face. 'Sit you down. My mother always said a good breakfast makes a good day.' Polly went to the stove to collect the porridge pot.

'Sorry, Polly, I'm not hungry,' Rosalind apologised.

'I know, my dear.' She nodded. 'It's just that you have to . . . to keep well for Livvy's sake. She's going to need you to be strong.'

At the small shake of Rosalind's head, she put the pan back on the stove.

'I really appreciate that you've put me up here so that I can stay near Livvy,' Rosalind said, picking up a slice of toast, more for appearances' sake than any desire to eat it.

'I knew she'd need you, as well as Beatrice, close to her until she's better,' Polly said practically. 'You had to stay somewhere in Lockhart. And better with me, where you and Beatrice can be together at this time.'

She watched Rosalind automatically scrape some butter on to the slice of toast.

'Has she got over the anaesthetic yet?' Polly asked.

'It was beginning to wear off yesterday.' Rosalind put down the knife.

'Such a young lass to lose her baby,' Polly said. 'But the doctor did say it wouldn't stop her having another child, didn't he?'

Rosalind nodded.

'He told Livvy and Donald that, but it's much too soon after the Caesarean section for them to be thinking that.'

'It's the doctor's way of helping them.' Polly tried to be comforting. She sat down opposite Rosalind. 'I feel so bad about Livvy's accident. That she should fall in the theatre. We should have warned her about the debris on the stage.'

'We don't know that's what she fell over,' Rosalind pointed out.

'Everyone at the theatre is blaming themselves,' Polly said. Rosalind didn't reply.

The door opened and Beatrice came into the kitchen. She slid into a kitchen chair without a word to anyone. Her hair hung lank on her shoulders, her sparkling blue eyes were dulled and the bloom had gone from her complexion.

'Good morning, love.' Polly immediately poured her a cup of tea, but Beatrice just stirred it with a spoon and didn't attempt to drink it.

Polly knew exactly how she and Rosalind felt. Nothing in the world seemed to matter, except the loss of a baby. The whole of the company felt the same.

'You'll be visiting today as usual?' she asked the sisters.

'The hospital has asked us to keep to the usual visiting hours from now on,' Rosalind said. 'Yesterday and the day before they let us in for most of the day.'

Polly took a long look at Beatrice, her heart going out to the young woman.

'I could use your help in wardrobe today, Beatrice, when you're not at the hospital. We need to make an inventory of costumes,' she said.

Beatrice looked up, horrified at the suggestion.

'I know that might sound uncaring but I feel if you involve yourself in something — ' Polly paused. 'Livvy is going to need both of you to support her through her recovery from the operation and the stillbirth.' She'd said the word that everyone had been avoiding. 'It doesn't mean that you are not grieving, instead it is an indication that you are trying to find a way to help.'

There was a long silence in the kitchen and Polly feared that she had antagonised the sisters completely.

'Actually, I think that's probably a good idea,' Rosalind said eventually. 'I've left Gil in the lurch with all the financial problems.'

'Donald said if we hadn't kept the theatre on, the baby would still be alive,' Beatrice blurted out.

'Yes, I know he said that,' her sister replied. 'At the moment it's his way of dealing with the grief. We all want something to blame.'

'Livvy could have fallen anywhere,' Polly said with sympathy in her voice.

'That's what she said herself — that it could have happened at home,' Rosalind said.

Beatrice began to cry.

Rosalind leaned over and put an arm round her shoulders.

'Remember what Livvy said yesterday. That she still believed in the theatre. It had nothing to do with the accident.'

Beatrice stopped crying and looked at Polly.

'She said that she'd been a passive owner for too long. If she'd visited the theatre earlier, she would have known much more about it and found her way around.'

Polly took Beatrice's hand.

'I think she probably said that to make us all feel better. She's a very special girl, that sister of yours. It's going to take her and Donald a long time to get over this, but maybe if she knows that both of you haven't given up on the Limelight it could go a little way to her recovery.'

★   ★   ★

Polly saw the appreciation and under-standing in Rosalind's eyes and felt reassured. At the moment, nobody at the theatre felt like doing anything, but they were forcing themselves to keep going, thinking it was the only way they had to show support for the sisters.

'I'm going to the Limelight as soon as I've seen Livvy this morning,' Rosalind said to Beatrice. 'It might be a good idea to take turns to visit today.'

'If you think so,' Beatrice murmured.

Polly surreptitiously spread butter and marmalade on a slice of toast and slid it across the table to Beatrice.

She wasn't sure she had said the right things. After all, she didn't really know the sisters all that well, or just exactly how the relationship worked between all three.

Her instinct suggested that at the moment they needed someone to hold them together. Whether it was her or not, she had no idea. But she knew she had to be there for them.

★　★　★

Gil was standing at the theatre office window when he saw Rosalind approach

185

across the square. Gone was her positive stride, her way of holding up her head at an angle as if enjoying everything she saw in her path.

Her shoulders were drooping, her eyes looking only at the next step in front of her. His thoughts had been with Livvy and Donald since Sunday, and he felt a knot of compassion in his throat.

He left the office to meet Rosalind. Impulsively, he held out his hands when they met and she briefly joined hers with his.

'You shouldn't have come here today,' he said gently.

'It was Polly's idea and I think she was right,' Rosalind replied, and they walked to the office. 'I've already seen Livvy this morning and Beatrice is with her now.'

'How is Livvy today?' he asked her.

Rosalind shook her head.

'Trying very hard to be brave. It's going to take a long time to . . . '

'It can't be measured in time,' Gil

said, standing back to let Rosalind enter the office first.

She nodded, then turned to the desk. He noticed she didn't want to talk further about the accident.

'Polly said the insurance assessor was here yesterday,' she said, her tone less muted.

'Yes, that's right, and I asked them to contact Andrew, as he has the policies.'

★　★　★

They sat down in chairs on opposite sides of the desk. 'He telephoned earlier this morning,' he continued. 'It's not good news. The long and short of it, Rosalind, is that we can only claim fifty per cent of the costs of repair. You'll remember the estimate from Bert Saunders?' He slid the sheet of paper across the desk.

Rosalind picked it up and read it again.

'Where on earth are we going to get enough money . . . ' Her voice trailed away.

'Andrew had some suggestions,' Gil said, trying to sound upbeat. 'Sponsorship from Glasgow companies, which he's tried already but thinks might be more successful now that the theatre itself is in danger of closing. Then he mentioned that we could apply for an historic building preservation order.'

Rosalind lifted her head and he noticed a gleam of determination in her expression.

'That sounds like a good idea. The Limelight is historically important in Lockhart. I'm sure all the local people will want to see it preserved. Its architecture is in harmony with the other buildings in the square. A modern building would ruin the whole ambience.'

'Shall I start making contacts?' he asked.

She gave him a brief smile.

'I'm here to work, Gil. I wouldn't want you to carry this whole burden. Andrew has given me leave of absence until I feel able to leave Livvy. Nicol wants me back in Glasgow as soon as possible, something to do with his new job, but that will have to wait.'

'Besides, Beatrice is here, too. Polly wants her in wardrobe for a little while today.'

'Oh, I'm not sure that's necessary,' Gil said.

'Maybe not for wardrobe, but I think Polly is right in encouraging Beatrice to keep in touch here. And it's what Livvy wants.'

'Really? I thought she and Donald would want nothing to do with the theatre.'

Rosalind shrugged.

'Donald won't come near here, but Livvy has told me privately that she wants no-one else to suffer because of the accident.'

'A very brave girl,' he said quietly.

Rosalind bowed her head.

'Yes, more than we all realised.'

* * *

After a quick cup of coffee, they each got down to business, tracking down as many possibilities for cash as they could find, taking turns to use the telephone.

After an hour, they stopped for a break.

'It's not looking very promising,' Rosalind said. Their pleas had been heard sympathetically, but no-one had put money on the table, so to speak. The Preservation Society had promised to send them a form to complete.

'We need to make more of an impact,' Gil said.

'We could ask the newspapers to run a feature with pictures of the Limelight over the years,' Rosalind suggested, 'and how it has been a civic amenity, explaining why we need money to help repair the storm damage. People might respond if they see what an architectural gem it is.'

'That's a brilliant idea,' Gil enthused. 'If we get enough money for the repair, we just might be able to cover our other expenses.'

They looked at each other, the beginning of hope evident on both faces.

'I'll search the archives for old photographs,' he said quickly.

'And I'll get on to the newspapers.' She reached for the telephone.

As he searched through the old files, Gil reflected that he and Rosalind really worked well together. They made a good team. Then he remembered Nicol. It was going to be very short-lived teamwork, and privately he dreaded the prospect of carrying on without her.

★ ★ ★

Andrew replaced the telephone on the stand. He'd spoken to Rosalind and heard the latest news of Livvy and also the funding ideas she and Gil were working on. They had high hopes concerning his suggestion of the preservation order.

Having promised to keep Avril up to date with developments, he telephoned her, too. She'd been rather subdued last time they spoke, very concerned for Livvy. He told her she was improving, then gave the other news from Lockhart.

'I've always had the highest regard for Gil Buchan, a thoroughly dependable type, and he has been lucky that Rosalind is such a dedicated owner,' she said over the receiver. 'I'm working on a new show for the opening night. And I hope Livvy and Donald will come along.'

He had one more call to make to a business associate.

'It's an architectural gem,' he told his contact a few moments later, unconsciously echoing Rosalind's description of the theatre.

He was still talking when the door to his office opened and Nicol was shown in. He waved him to a chair opposite his desk.

'The theatre is at the heart of the Lockhart community.' He continued with his call. 'You have to see it to appreciate that it's begging for preservation.' He paused as his associate spoke.

'I don't agree,' Andrew continued.

'Television is never going to replace live theatre, even if, as you imply, the Limelight is a little place in the sticks. That is the very reason why it is so important to keep it open. If you can see your way to make a contribution . . . ' After a few moments he ended the call.

'It makes me furious when people can't see beyond the big city!' he said to Nicol.

'It's the way the world is going,' Nicol replied.

'If we sweep away everything traditional we have no heritage.' Andrew was still bristling.

* * *

Andrew noticed that Nicol seemed more alert than usual. His easy good looks and charm were infused with suppressed excitement.

'I suppose that's one way of looking at it,' Nicol now said. 'But in Canada they look to the future with their innovations and modernisation. To be honest, Andrew, I wonder if the theatre is worth all this anguish, especially for Rosalind. She has enough to worry about with Livvy losing the baby.'

'Perhaps, but then Rosalind is not known for giving up on anything. She's been a good fighter on behalf of Jardine House for several years.'

Nicol crossed his legs and sat back in his chair.

'I'm going to try to persuade the girls to sell. In fact, only this morning I spoke to someone who is interested in buying.'

Andrew was astounded.

'In buying the theatre?'

'No, actually just the site.'

Andrew frowned.

'I hope you don't mean a property developer.'

Nicol leaned forward.

'You know that it will inevitably come to that, Andrew. And he'll pay a good price. There will be money for the girls and all the Limelight company. It will be like nice little pensions for everyone there.'

'But they don't want pensions,' Andrew said sharply. 'They want their jobs, to keep the theatre open. It's a lot more than nine to five for them, it's a way of life!'

'I understand that.' Nicol was genuinely sympathetic. 'I stayed in my job here in Scotland for years. It was only when I went on that temporary contract to Canada that I saw how things were changing in the world.'

'It could be that the theatre company is ready to move on, too. There will be new backstage jobs in television as it grows. Their expertise will be useful there.'

Andrew conceded that he did have a valid point over the jobs, but would the theatre company be prepared to up sticks and move to the city? He doubted that.

'You know, Andrew, with your business expertise you could persuade the girls to see the best option is to sell the theatre.'

Andrew studied his blotter. Having devoted himself for years to Jardine House, he'd just recently begun to realise that he'd missed the more emotional, personal contact with people. It was only when Rosalind had taken over the theatre that he'd become involved in her problems, albeit in an avuncular way, and somehow he'd come to admire Beatrice, too, and her commitment to achieving her ambition.

Perhaps, though, it was down to Avril, who'd somehow shown him the way to become involved, more caring. He found he enjoyed this wider aspect of his life and was happy to devote his energies to helping the theatre. He was about to explain some of this to Nicol, but the younger man spoke before he had a chance.

'I've just met my new company's representative who's over in Scotland this week. He has advised me that my starting date has been advanced so we'll be leaving for Canada very shortly.'

'Goodness. I thought that was several

weeks away. What about your wedding?'

Nicol's face was wreathed in smiles.

'That's going to be very soon. So, I reckon you ought to be interviewing folk for Rosalind's replacement. I'm on a high, Andrew, so excited. Rosalind will soon be my wife and we'll be off to the New World. I'm on my way now to Lockhart to give her the wonderful news.'

After he'd gone, Andrew worried over the implications of Nicol's announcement. Was there any chance of saving the theatre now? And what of Rosalind? She always liked to finish what she'd started. Did Nicol appreciate that? For a fleeting second he wondered just how well Nicol did know Rosalind's character.

Still, Gil was still there to carry on. Avril spoke very highly of his abilities and commitment.

The developers had to be the last option. Andrew searched his brain for some route that would hold off that event.

Then he smiled to himself. Could he

do it? Was emotion governing his idea?

Once again he reached for the telephone.

★ ★ ★

In a rather unsure frame of mind, Stuart made his way from Hillhead underground, walked past the BBC studios and then approached Avril Beaton's flat in Botanic Gardens Crescent. The whole crescent, rising high above the road beneath, was a semi-circle of elegant flats.

He felt completely out of his depth. He'd only come because Beatrice had insisted. Avril had telephoned her and said she wanted to see Stuart about a script.

Now, he clutched his folder of scripts and rang her doorbell.

★ ★ ★

Once inside, Avril chatted to him and he realised she was trying to put him at his ease. The flat was furnished with elegance and style, with a multitude of pictures, flamboyant shawls and a vast collection of hats.

'A daft little hobby, but I was once stuck for an appropriate hat in a play and had to go out and buy one. Now, I'm never at a loss.' She waved Stuart to a chair and produced a tray of coffee and biscuits.

He noticed that there were three cups on the tray.

'I should explain why I've asked you here,' she said, pouring coffee into two cups. 'I told Gil that I'd put on a show for the opening performance once the Limelight roof was repaired. I've asked Torry Dunbar to come tonight as I understand he's taken one of your scripts. I thought the three of us might work on a new show.'

Stuart let his folder slide down on the sofa.

'Miss Beaton . . . Avril . . . that was my very first script to be accepted. I'm a complete novice. I couldn't write material good enough for you.'

She smiled at him.

'Don't speak too soon! You have to understand that actors such as Torry and I need a constant supply of fresh material and I think we could shape your writing to suit our talents. The competition out there is fierce — and worse since television came along.'

Stuart took a sip of coffee. What she was suggesting would be fantastic. How often did writers get the chance to work with really experienced actors?

'I'd love to try, but . . . just at the moment I don't think my brain is at its inventive best.'

'Frankly, I'm not on top form, either,' she said, her fingers worrying the brim of a hat. 'The truth is I feel so responsible for Livvy's accident,' she said, her tone completely changed. 'You see, I was the one who suggested showing her round the theatre and when she eventually said she wanted to go back and find Donald, I didn't go with her!'

'Nobody blames you!' Stuart said at once.

'Except myself. If I'd been with her, I would have noticed the obstacles on the stage. I'll never forgive myself. And there's no way I can make things better for her. I've sent flowers and I'll visit when she's up to receiving visitors. I've never been in a situation like this and don't know how to handle it.'

Stuart sympathised. So far, all he'd done had been to try to comfort Beatrice. He had no experience of tragedy like this and had felt completely lost for words.

'All I can do is to help get the theatre on its feet again. I think Livvy would like that.' There was a question in Avril's voice.

Stuart didn't mention Donald's attitude.

'Yes, I think she would,' he said.

'It occurred to me that you might want to put your mind to doing something to help, too,' she said.

It dawned on him that Avril was more than just a successful actress looking for a new show — she had turned to him for help. He swallowed hard.

'I'll give it a go,' he managed to say.

★ ★ ★

Torry Dunbar looked amazed when he saw Stuart sitting in Avril's parlour, sipping coffee. She wasted no time in telling him of her idea.

'OK, let's see some of your material, Stuart.' Torry reached out for Stuart's folder.

He and Avril each took a handful of scripts.

'Hmm, good ideas, fresh approach, but some of your targets are all wrong,' Torry said kindly. 'You need to concentrate on a specific comedian as you did with the script I accepted.'

'That's why he's here,' Avril said. 'I thought the three of us could work together on a new show.'

'Do you have a venue in mind?' Torry asked.

Avril told him about the Limelight and her plan for an opening show.

'A little out of the way theatre like that — can they afford us?' Torry asked.

'Oh, come on, Torry, they've had a near disaster,' Avril declared. 'I'm putting this on for free.'

Torry got to his feet.

'Count me out on this one, Avril. I have a family to support. I need my performance fee every time. If I did a show for every good cause that asked, my family would be out on the street.'

No amount of persuasion on Avril's part could induce Torry even to consider a script and he left after another ten minutes.

'OK, Stuart, let's clear the decks and do this one on our own,' she said, removing the coffee tray.

Stuart was appalled. How could he just create a script for a whole show? He would need weeks to work on it — and Avril would want it in a couple of weeks to give her time to rehearse. He was terrified he was going to let everyone down.

He remembered Donald's comment when he met him outside the hospital.

'That theatre is jinxed!'

★　★　★

Rosalind tried hard to conceal her shock when she saw Livvy at the hospital after lunch.

Her sister's complexion was very pale and her normally rounded cheeks appeared to have shrunk dramatically. But it was her eyes that troubled Rosalind most. They were dull one moment and feverish the next.

She took Livvy's hand.

'Have you had your afternoon nap?' she asked.

'By order,' Livvy said with forced brightness. 'To tell the truth, I didn't sleep much. Donald has gone back to Glasgow to sort out some business matters.'

'Yes, he rang me at Polly's to make sure Beatrice and I would visit you today.'

Livvy shook her head.

'As if you wouldn't. He does fuss. I want him to stay in Glasgow. He can't neglect his business.'

'I agree,' Rosalind said. 'Anyway, the hospital will be discharging you soon.'

Livvy twisted the hem of the bed sheet.

'Yes, they did say tomorrow, but now they think I should stay a little longer.'

The unease that Rosalind had felt when she'd come into Livvy's room now deepened.

'Why is that?'

'Oh, probably nothing.' Livvy resumed her forced brightness. 'I'm just a little tired.'

'What did the doctor say?' Rosalind wasn't fooled.

'Oh, just something about complications.' She gave Rosalind a tight smile. 'Absolutely nothing to worry about, I'm sure. I'm just being lazy.'

Rosalind did her best to keep the conversation flowing with her sister, avoiding any medical chat, until visiting time was over for the afternoon.

'See you tonight.' Rosalind kissed her and left the room. She went straight to find a nurse.

'The doctor wants to speak to Mr Webster tonight,' the staff nurse told her. 'I'm afraid I can't tell you anything.'

Rosalind made her way back to the Limelight, sick with apprehension over Livvy's condition. She sought out Beatrice right away.

'How was Livvy when you saw her before lunch?' Beatrice asked, looking concerned.

Rosalind told her about the 'complications.'

'I think we should go back to the hospital tonight, even though Donald said he'd cover the visiting hour,' Rosalind suggested.

Beatrice said nothing but her hand, trembling, rested on Rosalind's arm for a second or two.

Rosalind went to the office to see if she could give Gil a break. He asked at once about Livvy, but she just said she was resting.

'Right, I will take up your offer of a break. Theatregoers also spend money in town so I'm going to speak to local shopkeepers. Some might be happy to make a donation. They won't want to lose custom.'

'Not much of a break, Gil,' Rosalind commented.

'I know them all. Maybe the personal touch will work.'

He'd no sooner left the office than Nicol arrived.

'Surprise!' He strode over to the desk and raised Rosalind from her chair. He took her in his arms and gave her the gentlest of hugs.

'How are you, my love?'

Rosalind rested her head on his shoulder for a moment, glad of his nearness and strength. She had missed him these last few days.

'Rather worried. Livvy is not so well.'

'Early days, my darling. She's in good hands.' He squeezed her hand. 'Anyway, I just had to see you. The most wonderful news which I couldn't possibly tell you over the phone.'

'What's that, Nicol?' she asked.

'Hold on to your hat — we're off to Canada sooner than we expected! My starting date has been advanced so, my dear one, there's just a little matter of arranging our wedding!' Nicol was beaming and then he picked her up and twirled her round the office.

'What do you mean?' Rosalind felt she was not thinking clearly. Of course, there would be their wedding, but that was not planned for a couple of months.

'Plans all changed, my darling. I have to start my new job in no less than three weeks' time, so it will take us a week to sail to Canada — it will be a great honeymoon.' He hugged her again. 'And that means we will have to get married in the next two weeks.'

Rosalind extricated herself from his arms.

'Nicol, my darling, there is no way I can arrange a wedding in two weeks' time — the church, the reception, the outfits . . . ' She felt as if she was in a parallel world — that her life was following two different paths.

'Sorry, Rosalind, my love, you'll have to forego all that. Special licence, registry office, that kind of thing.'

Rosalind felt a kind of paralysis seize her.

Yes, she could arrange a wedding in two weeks, but not now! Not in the next two weeks! How could she walk away from Livvy? How could she leave the theatre in such a state of uncertainty?

She looked at Nicol's loving, positive face and knew she had to make a decision.

7

Livvy smoothed the sheet under her hands, all the while taking a covert glance at Donald. He looked, she felt, much worse than she did. She knew her body was recovering from the Caesarean section, but still to come were the results from the tests the doctor had insisted on. He was due in her room any minute now.

'I feel so much better.' She leaned over to Donald's chair to take hold of his hand. 'It isn't going to be bad news.'

'No, I'm sure it isn't,' he replied.

She could hear the brave tone he'd forced into his voice. He was trying, as much as she, to be positive. For the present they had tried to bury the emotional devastation they suffered.

'Good morning.' The doctor swept into the room, a file under his arm.

'Good morning, Doctor Murray,'

Livvy said, and Donald echoed her.

The doctor took the chair on the other side of the bed from Donald.

'I'm sorry that the tests took so long but the results have now come through and I'm delighted to tell you that there is no serious problem with your health, Mrs Webster.' Dr Murray smiled at them both, though it was a gentle smile. He'd been with them all the way since they had arrived at the hospital the previous week.

'However — you do have a minor heart problem which, unfortunately, wasn't apparent during your pregnancy,' he said, looking at them both in turn.

Livvy glanced at Donald. He looked even paler than before.

'We think this caused you to faint at the theatre,' the doctor went on.

'You mean, I didn't trip?' Livvy asked.

Dr Murray shook his head.

'No, we believe there was a sudden fall in blood pressure, causing you to lose consciousness.'

'So it wasn't my fault.' Livvy felt tears of relief welling up in her eyes.

'Livvy! No-one said it was your fault,' Donald protested.

'No, of course not,' Dr Murray intervened quickly. 'It could have happened at any time. It occurs without warning. It might have happened when you were coming down stairs and you yourself could have been badly injured.'

Livvy leaned back against the pillows. They had not lost their son because of her carelessness. It was, in its way, a small comfort.

'Could this happen again?' Donald voice was still tight.

'Not now that we know the reason for Mrs Webster's collapse.' Dr Murray turned to Livvy. 'Your heartbeat has shown some irregularity in rhythm. This can be treated with medication and you will be fine, able to lead your life just as you have always done.'

'Thank you, doctor,' Livvy said quietly. 'For everything you've done.'

'I just wish we could have saved your baby.' He looked at both Livvy and Donald. 'But the shock of the fall . . . ' He paused. 'That won't happen again. You needn't be afraid of that.'

'It's much too soon, I know, for you to be thinking of . . . but I have to say there is no reason why you can't have children in the future.'

Livvy just nodded. It was much too soon to be thinking of that, but she was glad Donald had heard the doctor say it was possible. She wanted them to have a child eventually.

Dr Murray left them, saying that her heart medication would begin that day and once they were happy with her condition she would be discharged.

'Livvy,' Donald began as soon as they were alone again. 'I'm sorry if I made you feel bad about tripping in the theatre. I was so wrong to put the blame there. I just felt I had to find a reason. I didn't realise that you were blaming yourself.'

'It's behind us now, Donald. None of

us could have predicted what would happen. We will just make sure we never forget the son we might have had,' she said, taking his hand again.

Both were lost in those thoughts when there was a knock at the door and Rosalind and Beatrice came into the room.

At first, they looked shocked at their tear-stained faces.

'It's all right,' Livvy said quickly. 'I'm going to be fine.'

'The tests?' Rosalind asked.

Livvy repeated what Dr Murray had told her.

Donald got up from his chair to offer it to Rosalind.

'Make sure everyone at the Limelight knows it was nothing to do with the debris on the stage,' he said. 'I'm sure they are all blaming themselves.'

'We all felt responsible in some way,' Rosalind admitted.

'Right! Enough of this.' Livvy pushed back the bedclothes and gingerly swung her legs out of the bed.

'What are you doing?' Donald protested.

'I am not an invalid! I am determined to recover as soon as possible,' she said.

'Don't be too hasty. We've been so worried about you,' Beatrice said from the window, where she was arranging some flowers in a vase.

'I know, and you've no idea how comforting it has been to Donald and me having you both here in Lockhart with us,' Livvy said. 'And don't forget to thank Andrew for giving you all that time off to stay here, Rosalind.'

'No, I won't. He's been very understanding,' her sister murmured.

At that moment a nurse entered the room.

'Hello, Mrs Webster. I have your new medication here. Now I just need to take your blood pressure and pulse first. Perhaps your visitors would excuse us?'

Donald, Rosalind and Beatrice made to leave the room, but were stopped as Livvy called out.

'Don't worry, you three, you know I'll be sensible,' she assured them all. 'After all, there's going to be a wedding in this family soon and I intend to be there!'

*   *   *

Outside, the sun was beating down. It was a glorious day. Beatrice linked her arm through Rosalind's.

'Are you coming to the theatre?' she asked. 'I want to tell everyone about Livvy. They've all been so worried.'

Rosalind hesitated. She knew she should go there, especially as she had to return to Glasgow and Jardine House as soon as possible, but she needed some time on her own.

'I have one or two things to do in town. Tell everyone I'll call in later.' She planted a soft kiss on Beatrice's cheek.

Rosalind made her way down to the shore and began to walk along the beach, thinking about Livvy's news. She was so relieved it wasn't anything more complex. Nicol would be glad of that, too — if she had the chance to tell him.

She raised her eyes from the sand beneath her feet and realised she was close to the café where Nicol had proposed to her. What a wonderful night that had been! And now?

She felt shaky and made her way to a rock by the edge of the shore and sat down. She could recall every second of the last time she'd spoken to Nicol.

★   ★   ★

They'd been together in the theatre's office — a room that suddenly seemed to hedge them in. Nicol's face had been full of happy expectancy as he'd outlined his plans for a marriage within two weeks and then departure for Canada.

'Oh, Nicol, I don't think this is going to be possible,' she began as he waited for her agreement to his plans.

'What do you mean — not possible?' He sounded completely disbelieving.

'You do want to get married, don't you, my love?'

'Of course, Nicol, but I can't make plans just yet.'

'We don't have time to wait,' he warned.

'Nicol, darling, I can't leave Livvy at the moment,' she said. 'There's something wrong with her and she is having tests. She is not at all well. I can't leave until I know she's going to be all right. She might need my help for a while.'

'She has Donald and Beatrice to help her,' he pointed out, stroking her fingers. 'I know how close you girls have always been and I'm absolutely certain Livvy wouldn't want you to change our plans because of her.'

He was right, she knew that, but she wasn't going to tell Livvy about the imminent wedding. For one thing, in all probability Livvy would still be in hospital.

'There's nothing you can do for her, darling,' Nicol said gently. 'The doctors are there for that. Besides, I need you.'

'I accept all that. It's just that we don't know what's ahead of her.'

She'd always been protective of her sisters. As soon as she had been demobbed from the WAAF their mother had fallen sick and Rosalind had naturally taken on looking after her and mothering the girls at the same time. She could not walk away from Livvy at this time.

'We have so much time ahead of us, Nicol,' she said. 'We did originally plan a Christmas wedding, so why not go for that? I don't expect you'll have leave before then anyway, so you can fly over, and we'll get married and go back to Canada together.'

'Christmas! Rosalind, I don't want to wait that long. That means I'll be on my own for months!'

'I know, and I'll miss you terribly, but I think we need this time — at least it will help me, not only giving me peace of mind about Livvy, but arranging things here, selling the flat and such like.'

Nicol turned his head to gaze out of the office window.

'Ah, it's more than just Livvy, isn't it, Rosalind?' he said quietly.

'What do you mean?'

He turned to look at her.

'It's also to do with this theatre, isn't it? You want to sort it out before you leave.'

Rosalind smothered a sigh.

'No, the theatre doesn't come into it, Nicol. I'd never put that before you. Yes, there are lots of problems here, but Gil is more than capable of sorting them out. He doesn't need me.'

'You seem to think that everybody needs you except me, Rosalind.'

'That's not so. But if we work towards a Christmas wedding . . . '

Nicol got to his feet.

'I need you now, Rosalind! I leave for Canada in two weeks' time. Nothing can alter that.'

She saw the hurt and confusion in his face and her heart went out to him, but even as she rose from her chair, he left the office.

After a moment she went over to the window which overlooked the road. He was going towards the station to catch the train to Glasgow. She half raised her hand to wave to him but he didn't even look up, he just plodded on, his head down.

★ ★ ★

The keening of a seagull swooping over the beach brought her back to the present. She scooped up some sand and let it trickle through her fingers.

It was now two weeks since that day. She'd written to him, hoping she could explain her feelings better on paper than in a tense conversation. She'd told him how much she loved him, how she wanted to be his wife, but begged him to understand why she had to stay in Scotland at the present time. There had been no replies.

She couldn't believe that he didn't

want to see her again, but he'd made no attempt to telephone or meet her. Rosalind found it hard to accept that if he truly loved her he couldn't see her point of view.

★　★　★

With a sigh she retraced her steps along the beach and began to make for the theatre. To her surprise she saw Gil walking towards her.

'Hi. Beatrice saw you heading to the beach and I thought I'd come and join you,' he said. 'Great news about Livvy.'

'Yes, it is. I just needed a little time to think things over,' she said.

'Well, I have some news for you, but let's go somewhere else.' His smile looked concerned.

He guided her across Lockhart's square and into a narrow side street, then stopped at a small ice-cream parlour.

'Until you've tasted Luigi's creations, you don't know what ice-cream is.' He pushed open the door and they went inside.

He ordered a selection of flavours and insisted that she sample them all before he got down to talking.

'The good news is that the Preservation Society are happy to support us, but they can only give us a certain amount of money,' he told her.

'Is it enough for the roof repairs?' she asked.

'No. The bad news is that Bert Saunders won't begin the repair work until all the money is promised.'

Rosalind put down her spoon.

'We can't delay the repair or it will take ages to get the theatre up and running.'

Gil nodded.

'The longer the Limelight is closed the faster people forget, and it will be more difficult to attract theatre groups and audiences.'

'We have to find the money now,' she said, scooping up some ice-cream but failing to enjoy the taste. 'I'll apply for a bank loan.'

'The banks need some collateral before they promise,' he warned her. 'I checked that out myself.'

'I could provide my flat as collateral,' she said, thinking fast.

'You can't do that! There's Beatrice to think of.'

Rosalind smiled at him.

'You don't think for one minute now that Beatrice has a job here at the theatre that she's going to come back to Glasgow?'

'I guess not, but what if things went wrong and you lost all the money?'

'I'll make sure Beatrice's half share is safe.'

'Look, I'll put my house up, too,' Gil said. 'We're in this together.'

Rosalind was very touched by his offer. Whatever happened in the future with the theatre, Gil had a steely streak of loyalty all the way through.

'Thanks, Gil, I appreciate the offer, but I took on the Limelight and I don't want to see you homeless.'

She saw he was about to protest.

'I'll be selling my flat in the long run, anyway,' she said lightly, wondering, though, about the future and what it held.

'Oh, of course.' Gil nodded. 'I haven't seen Nicol for a week or so. Is he very busy?'

'Preparing for his new job,' she said casually.

'So, do you have a set date for leaving?'

Rosalind shook her head.

'Not yet.' She bent her head to the bowl of ice-cream so that Gil wouldn't see her face. According to the date burned in her brain, Nicol would have left for Canada that very morning.

* * *

Since it was such a lovely morning, Avril decided to walk through Glasgow's Botanic Gardens on her way to meet Beatrice and Stuart. The sun

225

glinted off the panes of glass which made the Kibble Palace such an outstanding feature of the Gardens. Being Saturday morning, families were picnicking on the grassy lawns.

She exited the park and made her way down Byres Road, then turned left up the hill to the girls' flat. Beatrice greeted her with a hug and Stuart immediately offered her a cup of coffee.

'I'm so glad to see you here, Beatrice,' Avril said.

'Rosalind and I came up from Lockhart yesterday with Livvy and Donald,' Beatrice told her. 'I'm not going back until Monday so Stuart and I can have some time together.'

'How is Livvy?' Avril asked.

'Tired after the journey, but otherwise fine.'

'I'll visit her as soon as she's had some rest,' Avril said. 'I'm really relieved her health problem has been resolved. If only it had been discovered . . . '

Beatrice nodded.

'Life can be very cruel.'

They went into the sitting room and Avril thought it was better to change the subject.

'Is Rosalind out with Nicol?' she asked.

'No, she's at work — on a Saturday! You know Rosalind. She's been away from Jardine House for two weeks now and thinks the place will have gone to ruin,' Beatrice said. 'Anyway, Nicol has left for Canada.'

'Oh, I see,' Avril said, but she was puzzled. Surely that was rather sudden? And didn't they plan to marry before he took up his new job? But Avril knew it wasn't her business, so she didn't ask any further questions.

Avril opened her capacious handbag and took out Stuart's scripts.

'These are just the ticket.' She smiled at him. 'You've written some excellent sketches which we can incorporate into the show for the reopening of the Limelight.'

'Gosh, really?' Stuart's grin was a mile wide.

'Let's run through some now,' Avril

went on. 'I'm not sure who we can engage to be my partner for the two-hander. I need to hear the lines in a different voice so that I can judge who might be suitable. Would you read the other part, Stuart?'

'Couldn't Beatrice do that?' he asked. 'I want to listen. It's only when someone reads my lines that I can hear if there's any rhythm to them. Beatrice has always read my stuff before I've sent it out to actors.'

'Very astute, young man.' Avril laughed. 'Beatrice, you're on!'

They pushed the sofa to one side to give them space to perform as if they were on stage.

The performances sparkled. Avril could feel herself responding to the situations Stuart had created, and the lines he'd given her were ideally suited for her stage personality.

But it was also a rather daunting revelation for her. Despite all her training and the vast number of shows she'd given over the past twenty-odd years, Avril was acutely aware that Beatrice was a superb performer.

Beatrice was a naturally gifted comedienne, her timing was perfect and it was clear she could take on the persona of any character Stuart had created. Her youth and energy dominated every scene and Avril felt she was outclassed. Beatrice, though, was quite unaware of this.

'Some things could work better,' Stuart said when they'd finished. 'I've made notes and will rewrite some lines.'

'You're the writer,' Avril said. 'I would like to perform them all. What about you, Beatrice?'

'Me?' She was surprised.

'I reckon we make a good pairing.' Avril barely paused. 'Actually, I'll put it to Gil that maybe the Limelight should try to become a repertory theatre, like Molly Urquhart's Rutherglen Rep. Taking part in that would be great training for you.'

Beatrice looked wistful.

'I'd love to, but I'm just an ASM at

the moment. I don't think Gil will let me act for a while.'

'We'll see,' Avril said. 'Of course, it might be some time before this comes about — until the roof is repaired for sure. Gil said you hadn't managed to get quite enough cash.'

'That's all fixed now, and work should start on Monday,' Beatrice said.

'That's marvellous! You'd better get down to those rewrites, Stuart,' Avril chivvied him.

'I'm amazed they got the money for the repairs so quickly,' Avril said as he walked her to the door.

He stepped outside on to the landing beside her.

'It was Rosalind who put up the balance,' he whispered. 'But she doesn't want anyone else to know.'

★ ★ ★

For his day out with Avril, Andrew had decided to take her to St Andrews. Apart from the fact that he loved the town, it would take them away from Glasgow and Lockhart and allow them to get to know one another better in privacy.

'Andrew, this is delightful,' she said as they stepped from the car in the centuries-old town. 'I was so pleased when you rang to invite me out. I tend to work on scripts when I'm alone at home.'

'You're rather like me, too much involved in work,' he said, hoping she'd see that they were of the same mind when it came to their professions. Surely that was a link between them?

'Mm.' She sounded a little non-committal.

Andrew decided it might be too soon to pursue that particular line of conversation. Instead, he escorted her along past the university and eventually they reached the ruins of St Andrews Cathedral. Avril seemed thrilled with their exploration, and their conversation was so easy and friendly that Andrew began to feel hopeful again.

Afterwards, he took her to a tearoom, redolent with images of times past, with panelled walls and leaded windows.

'This is such a treat, Andrew.' She leaned across the table towards him. 'So thoughtful of you to give me such a special day.'

'It's what I wanted for you,' Andrew replied, wondering if his responses were dull and lumpen. He wished he were more skilful in the art of — well, he supposed it was old-fashioned, but he thought of it as courting.

'To tell the truth, I've been a bit down recently,' she said, her voice low.

He was instantly concerned.

'That's not like you. Can you talk about it?'

She gave him a rueful smile.

'Frankly, I'm wondering if I'm past my prime in the theatre.'

'Never!' He almost spilled the tea in the force of his answer.

'You always see the best in people, Andrew, that's your special quality,' she went on before he could reply. 'It's been at the back of my mind for a while and then yesterday it hit me full on.'

He stared at her, confused.

'We had a run through of Stuart's scripts and Beatrice acted me off my feet.'

'Oh, come on, Avril, she can't be anything like half as good as you.'

She shook her head.

'But she is. She is a natural actress with great promise and, believe me, I have the experience and judgement to accept it.'

'Well, I don't,' he said stoutly. 'You are a star, such a popular entertainer, better than any of those young actresses.'

She gave him a rather winsome smile.

'A lady never reveals her age but I have more years behind me than Beatrice and . . . ' Her voice became soft. 'Livvy's sad experience made me think about my life. The way the family rallied round her was so marvellous. I don't have family. I've put everything into my career and lost something along the way.'

'I understand exactly what you

mean,' Andrew said, thinking this could be the opening he was hoping for. 'I, too, have missed out on so much for years.'

'By devoting your life to Jardine House?'

'Precisely. Like you, I have no family. Oh, I know all my staff and have learned about their families, but it isn't the same as belonging.'

'Look at the Forsyth family, such closeness, such strong bonds.' Now he had his chance to say what was closest to his heart. 'It would make my life perfect to have someone special to care for.'

Avril smiled at him.

'You spread your care around, Andrew. It's a wonderful characteristic.'

It wasn't quite the response he'd hoped for.

'I have to confess that I have done something that is rather selfish,' she went on. 'I suggested to Gil that he could set up a repertory company with me as one of the players — that would extend my stage life.'

'That sounds like a good idea once

the theatre repair goes ahead,' he said rather formally.

'Oh, it's all sorted as Rosalind has put up the remainder of the money.'

'What? How on earth will she pay for that?' Andrew was horrified.

Avril clapped her hand over her mouth.

'I've betrayed a trust in telling you that. I'm sorry — it just spilled out.'

Andrew sat back in his chair for a moment, then leaned over and patted Avril's hand.

'Don't worry, Avril. I've just been waiting to see what was needed for the theatre. Now I know what to do.'

Avril's eyes opened wide.

'What . . . ?'

'But you mustn't break my trust when you find out,' he said gently.

Later, when he took her home, he dared to place a gentle kiss on her cheek. Maybe he'd been trying to rush things with her. At least by helping the theatre he'd contribute to her happiness, which was what he wanted above all else.

He wanted to share that happiness with her, but still had no idea if she had any warmer feelings towards him at all.

★　★　★

Rosalind was relieved to be back at her desk in Jardine House. The last few weeks had been so tumultuous, but now she felt back in control.

'I'm so glad you're back.' Muriel, Andrew's secretary and her good friend, greeted her on the Monday morning. 'I've really missed you and felt so sorry for your sadness.'

Rosalind gave her a smile and a nod, accepting her sympathy.

'It may be too soon, but you've so much to look forward to in the future,' Muriel said, hoping to change the subject tactfully. 'Actually, I've picked out my bridesmaid's dress.'

Rosalind's stomach turned a quick somersault.

'It's still only August,' she said.

'I know, but you haven't told me the

exact date of the wedding.'

'Probably Christmas,' Rosalind murmured, opening a file, hoping her friend would take the hint. She had piles of work to catch up with, but mainly she wanted to stop this conversation.

'How's Nicol enjoying his new job?' Muriel chattered on.

'Oh, fine,' Rosalind lied, having heard nothing from him. There was a hollow feeling inside her and she could not talk about it. 'Give me time to sort out all this work, then we can get down to details.'

'Christmas,' Muriel mused. 'I think red velvet, perhaps. Something warm, anyway.'

Rosalind didn't lift her eyes from the tasks in front of her, but her concentration was all over the place. She'd written again to Nicol, telling him about Livvy and that she was looking forward to hearing from him about the job and how soon he'd get leave.

At lunchtime Rosalind slipped out to the bank. She'd telephoned them from

Lockhart on the Friday and set up the bank loan. All it required today was her signature. Although she didn't want the possibility of Beatrice being financially penalised, her sister had insisted.

'The theatre is my job now. If it closes, I'll never get another chance. I insist we share the cost,' Beatrice had pointed out.

'Ok, but I'll sign for it in the meantime.'

* * *

As soon as she got home that evening, Rosalind flopped on the sofa. The post had been but there was no airmail. She willed her thoughts not to dwell on Nicol's silence. She had to give him time.

The knock on the door surprised her. She was even more surprised to find Gil on the doorstep.

'Hello, sorry about the interruption. Well, no, I'm not.' He was beaming. 'I just had to bring this to you in person right away, otherwise you'd never believe me.'

She opened the door wide and they went into the kitchen. There, Gil reached into his jacket pocket, took out a piece of paper and laid it on the table.

Rosalind looked at it. It was a cheque. It was made out to the Limelight theatre and she got the shock of her life when she saw the amount.

'Gil? What . . . where . . . '

'Anonymous donor.' He then put a letter on the table.

It was from a firm of Ayrshire solicitors and informed them that their client had instructed them to send this amount anonymously to help with the restoration of the theatre.

'But this is far more than we need for the roof,' she whispered, unable to believe the evidence before her eyes.

'I know. It means we can replace the damaged stalls, seating and carpet and probably do a little redecorating.' Gil couldn't stop grinning.

'But who would give us this?' she asked.

'We clearly have a generous benefactor somewhere, probably in Lockhart, who believes in us.'

'We must write and express our thanks and gratitude immediately,' she said. 'And put a thank-you notice in the local paper, too.'

'Exactly my thoughts.' Gil leaned over the table and clasped Rosalind's hand. 'I can't believe we've been so lucky.'

Rosalind squeezed his hand in return, and then he withdrew it and his expression became unreadable.

'I suppose this means that you're free to go to Canada now,' he said.

Her mind went completely blank for a moment and then she felt a shiver of uncertainty possess her body. Was that what she really wanted?

8

'Who are you looking for?' Gil whispered to Rosalind. They were standing in the wings, and she was peeking round the end of the stage curtain.

'Our anonymous donor,' she replied.

'He isn't going to have 'benefactor' written on his forehead,' he teased her.

Rosalind withdrew her head and gave him a wry look.

'I'm trying to spot someone who looks serious and committed. I'm sure he's out front, this being our Gala Opening Night.'

'You're probably right. He must be a local man to give us this level of support, but he won't be flaunting his presence. He's insisted on anonymity from the beginning,' Gil reminded her.

'It would just be nice to thank him.' She let the curtain go.

Thanks to the unknown man not

only was the roof repaired but there were rows of new seating in the stalls, with new carpeting beneath, and there had even been enough money to give the whole auditorium a fresh coat of paint.

'It's nearly curtain up time — you'd better take your seat,' Gil warned.

Rosalind whispered the traditional good luck message 'Break a leg' to Gil and began to make her way from the wings. She had an aisle seat next to Livvy and Donald who were already there, together with Andrew.

Backstage, the air was humming with anticipation and excitement, although the experienced backstage staff were going about their business with calm expertise. It never failed to amaze Rosalind how everything fell into place, although she had long recognised that Gil, as director, commanded a good team.

It was with a start that she saw Beatrice walk towards the wings. Her sister's face was chalk white. What had gone wrong with her make-up? Beatrice was usually so particular about it, having trained at the beauty counter in Jardine House.

Rosalind whispered the good luck message to her sister, too, but she didn't even seem to notice or hear. Probably concentrating on her lines, Rosalind guessed.

Rosalind slipped into her seat, nerves tingling. It was a full house, booked well in advance. There was no doubt about it, the people of Lockhart loved their theatre. It was a miracle that it had been saved. If only she could tell the audience about how it had come about, but it was a condition of the gift that they were forbidden from mentioning it.

With a drum roll, the show got under way, and Rosalind sat back to enjoy it. That didn't last long.

The second act to perform was Avril and Beatrice in one of Stuart's sketches.

'What's wrong with Bea?' Livvy

whispered in her ear after a few minutes. 'She looks terrible.'

Like a lump of ice, Rosalind thought. Her sister's easy grace was missing, she seemed rooted to one spot on the stage and was saying her lines in a flat monotone.

Avril was flashing anxious looks in her direction and the build up to the pay-off lines of Stuart's comedy was missing.

Then Avril completely changed the script. Rosalind had listened to Beatrice rehearse it over and over and knew it line by line. With consummate professional ease, Avril ad-libbed, making Beatrice's lumpen performance part of the comedy and delivering lines that only required a 'yes' or 'no' answer from her.

Rosalind wept inside for Beatrice. This was her big chance and it seemed like she was throwing it away. She had worked so hard as assistant stage manager, at the same time constantly auditioning for Gil until he was satisfied she could perform on the legitimate stage. In engaging her to act in a professional show he'd opened the way for her to apply for Equity membership. Without the precious Equity card she would not have a professional career.

Muted applause rang out as Avril and Beatrice left the stage.

'Did she forget her lines?' Livvy asked Rosalind under the cover of the clapping.

'She must have done — and how to move and smile . . . ' Rosalind's voice trailed away.

'Hasn't she got another spot after the interval?'

Rosalind nodded.

'She should have time to run through that script before then.'

★ ★ ★

Although she knew it would be tense backstage, Rosalind could not stop herself from slipping round once the interval began. The first person she met was Gil.

He gave her a quick, knowing look.

'Stage fright.'

'What? She never suffered that when performing in her amateur shows,' she said.

Gil shrugged.

'She's been nervous all day. It's her first professional performance and it really just hit her.'

'Can I do anything to help?'

'Not really. I reckon it would be best if you left her alone at the moment. Avril's seen it happen to other performers. Don't worry, Rosalind, she'll get Beatrice through the next sketch.'

'What if it happens every time the curtain goes up?' she couldn't help asking, knowing a professional career meant everything to her sister.

Gil gave her a sympathetic look.

'She'll learn how to cope with it and she has all of us to help her.'

Still desperately worried, Rosalind went back to her seat and repeated

Gil's words to Livvy.

'So that's what it was. Just remember, our Beatrice hasn't let anything beat her yet.' Livvy paused and then, rather over-casually, changed the subject. 'I expect Nicol is delighted to hear that the theatre is saved.'

'He's so pleased that you are well again,' Rosalind answered a little hurriedly. In fact, that was all Nicol had said in his last brief letter. There had been no mention of the theatre or when he expected to have time off to come over to Scotland, or even any reference to their future marriage.

'So, have you fixed the wedding date?' Livvy asked.

Rosalind fiddled with her programme.

'Nothing set.'

'You are still getting married?' Livvy said sharply.

This time Rosalind twiddled her engagement ring round her finger. She so desperately wanted to talk to someone, but was it fair to burden

Livvy with her problems?

'If I thought that you let him go to Canada without you because I was ill . . . ' Livvy carried on, sounding worried.

Immediately, Rosalind turned to her sister.

'No, nothing like that. Time was too short to make arrangements.' She felt it was a justifiable white lie. 'Nicol is caught up in his new job and finding somewhere to live. We'll get round to the wedding when everything is settled.'

She had decided that was the only way she could interpret his brief letter, yet a chill of uncertainty and sense of loss pervaded her heart.

'So you won't be going in the near future?' Livvy persisted.

Rosalind shook her head.

'Have you told Gil?'

'It's all been a bit uncertain,' Rosalind prevaricated.

'He should know your plans. He's part of all this — a big part. We couldn't have kept the theatre on without him — even before the storm.'

At that moment the lights went down and the curtain rose on the second half of the show. Rosalind knew that Livvy was right. She would sort it out with Gil. He deserved to know.

★　★　★

Anxiety over Beatrice surfaced again, but Avril had dealt with the problem. Beatrice's second performance was better, although it lacked the sparkle they associated with her.

They went backstage after the show but stopped outside the dressing room. From the raised voices inside it was obvious that Beatrice and Stuart were having an argument.

'You knew those lines word perfect and the sketch still fell on its face. My script went right out of the window! What went wrong?' he was asking her.

'I got stage fright, OK!' Beatrice's voice was an octave higher than usual. 'It happens.'

'What? After all those years on the stage?'

'It's a bit different when you're facing an audience, expecting a professional performance — and acting with a star like Avril. You have heard of first-night nerves?'

'Not when you're concerned. What if it happens again?' he asked.

'Don't be so negative, Stuart. I've got this far and I'm not giving up now.'

With that, Beatrice appeared from the dressing room and saw her sisters.

'No doubt you're thinking that if I'd gone to drama college this would never have happened.' She glared at Rosalind and swept past her.

Polly passed Beatrice in the passage but kept her head down until she reached Rosalind and Livvy.

'It's been a terrible shock for her.' Polly laid a hand on Rosalind's arm. 'Leave her be for the moment.'

'Yes, I expect it has.' Rosalind sighed, her heart heavy. Beatrice would see it as all her dreams in tatters on the first night!

'Actually, I wanted to speak to you, Rosalind,' Polly said after a moment. 'I have something of a problem, too . . . '

★   ★   ★

'Was I a good drunk?' Rosalind looked at Avril over the coffee pot and burst out laughing.

'I have never seen anything so funny in my whole life,' she told her. 'And the audience was in stitches, too. It was a brilliant performance.'

'I don't expect you've seen such a naughty play before. When Noël Coward first presented 'Fallen Angels' in the nineteen-twenties everyone was shocked, but he re-wrote it last year and toned it down.'

'Not enough to spoil the fun.' Rosalind was still grinning at the memory of Avril's performance. Her comic timing was nothing short of genius.

'I reckon Gil took a chance on presenting it here, but it seems to have paid off. He does know what he's doing.'

'A few more like that is what we want,' Rosalind said.

It was four weeks after the Gala Opening and the repertory season was in full swing. Avril had invited Rosalind to have coffee with her in Lockhart's Italian café.

Avril sighed.

'Not everyone would agree with you.'

'What do you mean?'

'Andrew was more than a little shocked at my performance.'

'Oh, come on, Avril, he must have seen how clever and inventive you were in that part.'

'It's not that. It's because I played a woman who drank to excess.'

'Andrew had a similar education to me,' Rosalind said at once. 'We were taught about more familiar traditional Scottish plays and classics. He needs time to get used to something rather daring and challenging.'

'I'm pretty certain he's in love with me,' Avril said, after a pause.

Rosalind put down her coffee cup and reached across to grasp Avril's hand.

'But that's marvellous! Although it isn't a surprise to me, as he's always talking about you. I've been hoping for years he'd find the right person.'

'Ah, that's the problem. I don't think I am the right person.'

Rosalind was about to protest when Avril held up her hand.

'Andrew would prefer me to take only 'nice' parts such as a grande dame or dignified lady, like the role I performed in Stuart's script on the opening night.

'I can do that, but I'm basically a jobbing actor, taking on a range of parts and comedies especially, sometimes being as common as muck. That's fun! I can't pretend I'm something I'm not.'

'And you?' Rosalind said softly. 'How do you feel about Andrew?'

Avril fiddled with her spoon.

'He's the kindest, most caring person I've ever met. And yes, I do love him. But what if I'm all wrong for him? What if eventually it doesn't work out? The last thing I want to do is hurt him. That's why I'm going to stop seeing him!' she said, pretending not to see. Rosalind's distraught expression.

★ ★ ★

'Stand still, for goodness' sake, Beatrice,' Livvy said, reaching out for her pincushion.

'You are so bossy,' her sister answered.

'If I do a job, I do it properly.'

'Polly doesn't behave like this,' Beatrice retorted.

'Polly's had years of experience with difficult actresses like you,' Livvy said. 'I'm just a learner.'

Beatrice groaned.

'How soon do you think she'll be back?'

'Thanks for the vote of confidence.'

Livvy had pinned the costume to mould round Beatrice's figure and was now threading her needle. 'She phoned yesterday to say her daughter is on the mend.'

'I'll be glad when she's home again.'

'Beatrice, you might not have noticed, but I'm actually doing a good job as wardrobe mistress,' Livvy told her.

Livvy was so glad she'd been standing beside Rosalind on Gala Night when Polly explained her problem concerning her daughter in London, who had fallen ill and really needed her there for a spell.

Rosalind had barely had time to ask Polly if she knew where they could find a temporary replacement for her when Livvy had immediately offered to do the job.

'I'm a good seamstress,' she'd told Polly. 'And if you leave me as many instructions as you can think of, I'm sure I'll cope.'

Polly had looked straight into Livvy's eyes and had smiled.

'I'd be delighted to leave you in charge.'

Since Livvy had left the hospital in Lockhart, she'd spent as much time as she could at the theatre and a friendship had sprung up between the two women. Despite her flamboyant dress and manner, Polly had a deep core of sensitivity and understanding of human nature. Livvy knew the older woman was perhaps the only one to understand how much she needed to involve herself in something absorbing to counteract her grief.

'Sorry, I'm just being a grump today,' Beatrice said now. 'See you later.'

The door of Wardrobe had barely closed behind Beatrice when it swung open again and Donald entered. Livvy felt a flutter of alarm. Although she'd been trying to find the right words to explain her feelings to him, she wasn't quite ready, especially now when she saw the set expression on his face.

'Well, here's my wife!' he said.

It wasn't a good beginning.

'Of course, silly, you know where you'd find me.' Livvy left her chair and moved over to hug him. His body felt tense and unyielding.

'I've missed you, Donald,' she murmured. 'How was your Highland tour?'

'It was cold in Inverness and I felt it even more when I got home to a cold, empty house.'

Now was not the time to remind him that he'd agreed she should stay in Polly's house with Beatrice while the wardrobe mistress was away.

'I wish I could travel up and down from Glasgow every day, but I'm needed here at the moment,' she said.

'Well, I'm really fed up with this situation,' Donald said. He'd moved away from her and was standing by the sewing-machine. 'It's not natural being on my own in our home. I want to see my wife after a long day working. I need you there, waiting for me when I come home.'

The time had come, whether she could find the right words or not.

'That's just it, Donald,' she said, after a pause. 'When you come home, I'll have been in the house all day. Alone. Time passed quickly before . . . when I was preparing for the baby, but now time stands still.'

Donald's face paled as he stared at her.

'I can't bear it,' she said, her voice shaking a little. 'I need something to take up my attention.' She hoped Donald would see it was just another way of explaining the emptiness that was at the heart of her life when she was alone.

He crossed the room and gently put his arms around her.

'I . . . I never thought . . . It didn't occur to me.' His voice was unsteady.

They stood embracing for several minutes, unable to speak.

'When Polly comes back and you're able to come home again, we'll do things together. You can come out with me on the coach tours.'

That was not the answer she wanted,

but how could she tell him?

'It's an idea,' she said, trying to sound supportive. 'Look, why not stay here in Lockhart tonight with me? I know it will mean an early start tomorrow for you to get back to Glasgow, but we'll have some time together.'

Later, as he slept peacefully beside her, Livvy's thoughts were troubled. She loved Donald dearly but she wanted to be here, in Lockhart, working in the theatre. She'd never fill the empty space where their son should be, but she had found being involved in the Limelight was good for her. The plain truth was that she didn't want to go back to Glasgow. But what was she doing to their marriage?

★　★　★

'You look like a kid who's off on a treat,' Gil said as Rosalind settled into the railway carriage beside him.

'This *is* a treat,' she told him. 'A

259

whole weekend off and seeing a couple of shows besides.'

He was glad he'd asked her to come with him to Aberdeen. She worked all the time — five days with Andrew and then spent the weekends at Lockhart.

'It's time we found some new shows for the Limelight and this is the only way to do it,' Gil declared positively.

'Goody, a lot to look forward to.' She grinned at him.

Gil wasn't sure when it had happened, but the business — like Rosalind he'd first met was now so much more relaxed and full of fun. It was amazing, considering the crises they'd weathered.

'So, you'll be around for some future shows, then?' He raised his eyebrows at her.

'Yes, I reckon so. No immediate plans to leave for Canada.' She avoided his eye.

'Well, I certainly wouldn't have left my girl behind,' he said bluntly.

Rosalind's head jerked up and she stared at him. He expected a sharp rebuke but instead was dismayed to see a dull flush colour her cheeks.

It was too late to withdraw his remark. Besides, it was what he genuinely felt.

'Nicol's busy with the new job and finding somewhere to live.' She looked out of the carriage window as the train sped up.

Something was off-key, he thought. Livvy was well again, the theatre had been saved, so to all intents and purposes Rosalind was free to go. Why couldn't she and Nicol look for a house together?

Looking at her face again, he was angry with himself. She looked pale and withdrawn. He'd probably fouled up the whole weekend by speaking his mind. But he wouldn't have left his girl behind — especially not a girl like Rosalind.

He'd no ulterior motive in asking Rosalind to accompany him to Aberdeen. He wasn't trying to take her away from Nicol. He wasn't that type of man. While he'd always thought Nicol wasn't nearly good enough for her, she had to make up her own mind about him.

Rather desperately he searched around in his mind for some topic of conversation that might make things more companionable.

'I'm trying to educate Andrew in being more open-minded about plays,' she said, out of the blue. Then she told him about Andrew's reaction to Avril's adept performance as a drunken lady.

'She was brilliant.' Gil seized on the chance to steer the talk away from personal matters. 'It takes a superb actress to deliver Noël Coward's lines.'

To his delight and relief, it appeared that Rosalind wanted to concentrate on the purpose of the weekend and Nicol wasn't referred to again. She seemed as lighthearted as when they'd met in the station.

They briefly discussed Beatrice's wish to undertake more stage management.

'You must have confidence in her since you've left her in charge this weekend,' she said.

'I think she's found exactly what she wants to do,' he said.

But they soon forgot about Lockhart and began to talk about themselves. Despite the overcast conditions they opted for a walk on the beach on the Saturday morning.

'Reminds me of all those Scout camps I went to. Windy, cold and usually wet,' Gil said.

'My first Guide camp was not in the least adventurous,' Rosalind recalled. 'We travelled to the site just outside Glasgow by tramcar!'

'Softies,' Gil said, with a serious face, before they both burst out laughing.

They ate their fish and chips lunch from newspapers as they walked along. Then they went to a matinée.

Over dinner later, they swapped stories of their services in the war, trying to top each story over mishaps and disasters.

'Like to come with me to the theatre in Dumfries next weekend?' Gil asked as the train headed towards Glasgow on Sunday afternoon.

'I certainly would, Gil.' Rosalind smiled at him. 'This has been a great trip.'

It had been fun and more than that for him. He suspected that Rosalind had made a special effort for him, although she must be troubled over Nicol's attitude. He was skating on thin ice, though. She could leave for Canada some time in the near future.

And that would leave him completely bereft.

★ ★ ★

Rosalind packed her bag for the trip to Dumfries the following week, aware of how much she was looking forward to spending more time in Gil's company. Last weekend had been, just as she had said, a real treat.

Gil's comment about Nicol leaving her behind had dominated her thoughts all week. Was she refusing to face up to the fact that Nicol seemed to be distancing himself from her? Or was that just his way of trying to make her join him in Canada, and that he didn't want to come back to Scotland for a wedding here?

Surely she should know her fiancé better than that? Memories of the weekend with Gil flooded back. She'd got to know much more about him than she'd ever known about Nicol. In fact, she and Nicol had rarely talked like that. Before he went to Canada theirs had been not much more than a companionable relationship.

When he'd come back from Canada so unexpectedly she'd been thrilled, especially when he proposed. She had been so sure she loved him, but now wondered if she'd been swept up in the romance of the situation. And she wondered just how well he knew her.

He seemed only to see her in terms of being his fiancée, with no other commitments to family.

She felt disloyal thinking those thoughts, especially when Nicol was not here to defend himself, but he could hardly expect her to sit at home waiting for his call to Canada. No, she was going to Dumfries with Gil and intended to enjoy herself.

★   ★   ★

'Let's live it up again. Fancy another fish supper?' Gil asked when they arrived at the town.

Rosalind laughed, agreeing. Their conversation and easy repartee just took up where they left off last Sunday.

Later that evening as they were leaving the theatre, they ran into a man, clearly waiting to speak to Gil.

'Gil! Good to see you,' he greeted him. He was tall with strong features and sported carefully styled hair. His dress was casual but he exuded an air of confidence and authority.

'Ian? Good grief, it is you, Ramsay!' Gil shook hands with the man and introduced him to Rosalind.

'Ian and I started in theatre way back, but he's now a bigwig in television,' he told her.

'For my sins!' Ian Ramsay smiled down at Rosalind, then turned back to Gil. 'Where were you last weekend? I went to the show at the Limelight. Not bad at all for a country theatre. I went backstage to have a word with Avril Beaton, worked with her once, and while on the premises I took the chance to do a bit of a recce.'

'Researchers tell us that viewers like to see our performers in the flesh, so to speak, and that increases their enjoyment of the television show next time they see it.' Ian bestowed a confidential smile on Rosalind. 'I produce the television series 'Islands Of Myth And Mystery'.'

'I've watched that a couple of times,' Rosalind said. 'It's something different.'

'I sized up your little place and it seems to fit the bill,' Ian went on airily. 'So, Gil, book me in for a week, say late October, just before our series appears on the screens again.'

'Actually, it's Rosalind's 'little place', and while I book the acts, this isn't our thing,' Gil told him plainly.

Ian immediately switched his attention to Rosalind.

'You won't believe the money we'll pay for this. No-one in their right senses would reject us. It will put you on the map and we'll employ your technical staff at our television rates.'

'Give us some time to think about this,' she said.

'No problem.' And with that, Ian tipped an imaginary hat and disappeared into the Dumfries night.

* * *

A wind that was building up to be a gale almost set Rosalind reeling as she stepped off the train at Lockhart on

Friday evening a few weeks later. Rain was lashing the platform but suddenly Gil was in front of her, taking her arm and leading her out of the station.

'Thanks for coming so quickly,' he said.

'Andrew let me leave work early so that we could deal with this,' she said.

'Let's go to the Urquhart Arms. We won't be disturbed there.' Gil tucked her arm firmly in his as they struggled against the wind.

Soon they were settled in a corner of the dining room and Gil had ordered a meal.

Agreeing to Ian Ramsay's booking had given them some headaches. Both felt presenting the television show was contradictory to the tradition of their theatre, yet the money had the promise of making their finances more secure.

And so it had proved. The stage versions of the television series played to packed houses every night and the revenue was all the Limelight's to keep.

But now it appeared as if the success

was back-firing on them.

'Did you tell Andrew about this?' he asked as they waited for the meal.

'He overheard part of our telephone call,' Rosalind confessed, 'in particular my saying to you, 'What on earth are we going to do this time?' '

'And he wanted to know if it was another disaster?'

Rosalind nodded.

'I told him that the television company wants to buy the theatre, lock, stock and barrel, and convert it into a television studio.'

'What did he say to that?'

'He was furious.' She paused. 'Told me we couldn't accept the offer as it would be a break with tradition in Lockhart and deprive the community of the theatre they've supported for years, and especially during the recent troubles.'

'He's got a valid point,' Gil agreed.

'I didn't tell him that offer included employing and training all our staff, plus paying them more than we do.'

'There's something else,' Gil said.

'Oh, no, Gil, not another crisis.' She accepted the plate of soup from the waitress with a wan smile.

'Not a crisis, but a twist to the problem.' He reached into his jacket pocket and drew out a letter. 'This came this afternoon while you were on your way here.'

She opened it and saw it was from the firm of solicitors who'd forwarded the cheque from the anonymous donor. The message was clear. His client had given the donation to keep the theatre going, not to see it sold.

'Whatever way it goes it looks as if we're letting someone down. This person thinks we have a moral obligation not to sell,' she said.

Gil nodded.

'But we also have a moral obligation to think of the best interest of the company, too.'

'I don't think I could bear to lose the theatre after all we've been through.' Her voice shook.

Gil briefly covered her hand with his.

'The thought devastates me, too.'

Rosalind held on to his hand. The Limelight was Gil's whole life. He had so much more to lose than she.

They finished their meal. Rosalind was to spend the night with Livvy and Beatrice and put them in the picture. On Saturday, once the company had arrived for the day's performances, they'd spell out the situation to them all.

'It's going to come as a shock to them,' she said as they parted.

★　★　★

The next day, Gil phoned Rosalind early on Saturday to say that Jock had told him the television company had already spoken privately to some of the company, offering them jobs if the sale went ahead.

'We've no idea who will take up the offer, or who wants to stay?' Rosalind asked him.

'Not yet,' came his grim reply.

Later, she and Gil, together with Livvy and Beatrice, faced the company on the Limelight stage.

'I gather it's not news to you that the television company want to buy the theatre for conversion to a television studio and employ many of you . . . ' Rosalind paused. 'We can't deny it's a good offer and we will not stand in anyone's way if that's what they want.'

Gil stepped forward.

'We decided the best way is to take a straight vote. Hands up those who want . . . '

Rosalind closed her eyes, blanking out the sea of faces in front of her.

If the majority opted for the television company, in a matter of minutes the Limelight would cease to exist.

9

'He's behind you!' A hundred children's voices screamed at the stage.

'Where? Where? I can't see him!' the principal boy cried as the villain of the pantomime kept dodging him.

'Maybe you shouldn't have come to the children's matinée,' Beatrice said to Andrew Jardine a few minutes later as the curtain came down for the interval.

'It was the only performance I could get a ticket for,' he explained. 'But to be honest, if anything proves the value of this theatre, it's the response of this audience.'

'And all the others,' Beatrice went on. 'Word has spread that there's a grand pantomime at the Limelight, due in no small measure to Donald bringing coachloads of audiences from all over the south of Scotland.'

'It's one I haven't heard of.' Andrew

consulted his programme. ' 'Locky's Lucky Charm'.'

'Written by Stuart especially for us,' Beatrice said proudly. 'Locky is short for Lockhart, and he has to find the lucky charm that will save the heroine from being thrown out of her home. A Cinderella story with a little difference.'

'Stuart wrote the script? Well, he certainly has come on.' Andrew looked at the cast list. 'I see that Avril is the Fairy Godmother. Does she appear soon?'

'Yes, she's in the second act and she has a stunning costume,' Beatrice assured him, fairly certain that Avril was the reason Andrew had come to the pantomime in the first place.

Rosalind had told Beatrice that they hadn't been seeing much of each other for a while and the romance seemed to have cooled off, by Avril's choice. It was a great pity. Beatrice sensed that Andrew was a lonely man.

'Mind you, there would have been no

pantomime at all if it wasn't for you,' she said.

'What do you mean?' Andrew's voice was sharp.

'When you told us about the television company's real intentions,' Beatrice replied. She would never forget that moment several weeks ago when Rosalind had stood on the stage asking the company to make the choice between saving the theatre and selling it to the television company.

There had been silence for almost a full minute. The company had shuffled about the stage, each one waiting for someone else to make the first decision. Then the door to the auditorium had burst open and everyone had been startled to see Andrew Jardine stride down the aisle.

Although he was known to the company as a regular member of the audience, most could not understand why he'd come at this particular moment. Beatrice had glanced at Rosalind.

'I told him about this meeting,' Rosalind had murmured. 'He wouldn't be here unless it was relevant.'

'Forgive me for appearing to interrupt you all, but I think it's very important that you do nothing until you hear what I have to say.' Andrew had climbed the steps on to the stage.

'I met a friend this morning to discuss some property acquisitions. In the course of the meeting he asked if I'd heard about the television company taking over the Limelight. He knows I have connections here.' He'd paused for a moment. 'He understands that the company has abandoned plans to convert the theatre to a television studio and instead plans to demolish it and sell the site to a property developer.'

'But they want a television studio!' Jock Simpson had declared.

Andrew had nodded grimly.

'Oh, yes, but the money they will get from the developer will allow them to build a state of the art studio in Scotland's central belt.'

Instantly a murmur of protests and questions had erupted from the company.

Andrew had held up his hand.

'Clearly I have no proof of this as the TV company is keeping quiet about it, but I think you should be aware of their plans.'

'But we've been promised jobs in television!' someone else had complained.

'That's not going to happen now, here in Lockhart, is it?' Jock had been angry.

'I think we all need time to digest this,' Rosalind had said and looked at Beatrice and Gil, who both nodded. 'What if we get together again tomorrow afternoon? We'll all have had time to think over this development.'

Next day, the decision was taken to turn down the offer from the television company.

★ ★ ★

Andrew brought Beatrice back to the present.

'Rosalind told me later that just a few company members left to work in television,' he said.

Beatrice nodded.

'Yes, there were some good jobs on offer in Glasgow, and the company has set up training schemes, too, but most folk didn't want to leave Lockhart or lose the theatre building. We've employed some new staff and the company is running much as usual now.'

'I haven't been here for a while,' he said reflectively. 'It's good to be back.'

Later, backstage, Beatrice repeated some of their conversation to Rosalind.

'He hasn't been here because Avril went away for a few weeks with that touring company,' Rosalind reminded her.

'To put some space between herself and Andrew?' Beatrice asked.

'She was worried that he was getting too keen and that she wasn't right for him. Frankly, I suspect she missed us all here — and probably Andrew, too.'

'It was smart of Gil to invite her to

take part in our panto. After all, she is very popular in Lockhart.'

Rosalind nodded.

'She brings in the audiences for sure, but I have to say, Bea, Stuart's script is first class. The children are involved up to the hilt and there are some really good jokes for the grown-ups.'

'It's been a real boost for his confidence,' Beatrice agreed. 'And he's been approached by some other comedians for material.'

'That's great news. That's always been his ambition.'

'Yes, he's ready to stand on his own two feet now,' Beatrice said.

Her sister turned and stared at her.

'Am I missing something here?' Rosalind's voice was sharp.

Beatrice shrugged.

'Stuart has been rather dependent on me. Now he's proved he can make his own way.'

Rosalind said nothing, although Beatrice could see the puzzlement in her eyes. But now was not the time to mention her plan, especially as her sister probably wouldn't like it, although it was too late to cancel.

★　★　★

'If you two have nothing better to do then please get out of the way.' Livvy bustled between them, a gorgeous satin dress draped over her arm. 'Avril needs this pronto.'

Rosalind and Beatrice melted away.

Livvy knocked on Avril's dressing-room door.

'Come on in, Livvy.'

She opened the door as wide as possible to carry in the gown without crushing it. She'd just spent an hour ironing the costume. It wasn't until she was properly in the room that she saw Andrew sitting in the armchair.

'Oh, sorry, I didn't know you had a visitor,' she began.

He got up from his chair at once.

'I'm just leaving, Livvy. It's nearly time for the curtain to go up again.'

He turned to look at Avril.

'I'm looking forward to your performance.'

'Thank you, Andrew. It's good to see you again.' There wasn't the usual confidence in Avril's tone and Livvy noticed she was fussing with a powder puff.

'And you,' he said, but his voice sounded forlorn.

Livvy had the distinct impression that she'd walked in at exactly the wrong moment and that, given more time alone, Andrew and Avril might just have been on the verge of restoring their friendship. But she'd had no choice. She was in charge of Avril's wardrobe and it was time she was in costume as the interval was almost over.

★ ★ ★

Late on Christmas night, Rosalind returned to her flat in Glasgow. She sat at the window, looking at the starry sky. Her Christmas wedding plans had not materialised. Nicol had not come back for her.

She slipped the engagement ring from her finger. She would write to him, breaking off the engagement, posting back his ring and asking for his forgiveness. She thought back to that day in Lockhart when he'd suddenly appeared at the theatre. She'd loved him then, hadn't she?

Until then their relationship had been grounded in friendship, and maybe the initial parting had led her to think that it was love when he returned.

She wrote to him that night and parcelled up the ring.

★ ★ ★

It was early January when he replied. It was the longest letter he'd written since he'd gone to Canada. It was the most gentle one he'd written, too.

He said he knew he'd been selfish in insisting on the quick marriage and asking her to leave her family at a time of illness. Over time he'd come to accept that their love was not meant to be. It was no-one's fault. They perhaps should have remained just friends.

He then confessed that he'd met someone else, a Canadian girl, and he'd been on the point of asking Rosalind to release him from the engagement.

Rosalind wept a few tears for something lost, but was glad that Nicol had found happiness with someone else.

She walked round the flat. She had not told anyone that she now owned it. She thought back to the time she'd made the sudden decision to buy it. Nicol had gone off to Canada, Beatrice to Lockhart.

She'd felt insecure and had used the money she'd saved for Beatrice's drama college fees as a down payment and set up a mortgage. She wondered if she had subconsciously realised at the time that she'd never go to Canada.

When she told her sisters about the end of her engagement to Nicol she would have to confess about the flat. It would always be there for Beatrice, of course, should she need it, but Rosalind was certain that her sister had found her dream niche in Lockhart.

★ ★ ★

January and February were lean months for the Limelight as people tended not to go out so much on cold evenings. Donald's touring business was curtailed, too.

'Are you sure you still need to be at the theatre all week?' he grumbled to Livvy as they were having lunch during his usual weekend visit to Lockhart.

'We need this quiet time to catch up on repairs to the costumes and to search out new patterns,' she explained. 'I've been taking a dress-making class in my spare time. I just love this work.'

'Aye, I can see that, but I'm fed up being a weekend husband.'

Livvy pushed her plate away.

'I've been worried about you in

Glasgow during the week, love, but I think I have a solution.'

'You're coming home?' He took her hands in his.

'Home is what I'm talking about, Donald. We could have one here in Lockhart. There's a bungalow up for sale not far from Polly's house.'

'I walk past it every day and I think it would suit us just fine. It has quite a bit of land behind it, where you could build a garage and move the coach business to Lockhart.' She stopped, quite breathless.

Donald withdrew his hands.

'Oh, Livvy, I don't know. It seems such a big step. I'll need time to think about it.'

'Of course, I know that, but not for too long because there's something else now.'

'Nothing else, Livvy, that's enough planning for the moment.' He frowned. 'Anyway, our flat in Glasgow is just right for us. A bungalow is a big commitment.'

She took his hands firmly in hers.

'We're going to need the space.'

It took a few seconds for Donald's frown to clear as he strove to understand her words, then she saw the light of joy in his eyes.

'You mean . . . ?'

'Yes, the doctor confirmed it only yesterday. The baby is due in August!'

★　★　★

By Easter the theatre was playing to full houses again. Andrew's information had proved correct and the newspapers were full of the spanking new television studio taking shape in Glasgow.

Gil and Rosalind were spending more time together, making regular visits to theatres to choose new shows and taking the opportunity to have bracing walks along Lockhart's shore, talking about everything under the sun.

Just after Christmas, he'd noticed that she'd stopped wearing her engagement ring. He'd said nothing, not sure whether she was heartbroken or not. The side of Rosalind's character that contrasted with her business expertise was very private and, he guessed, sensitive. He didn't want to say anything about his feelings until the right moment arrived, but he knew she was enjoying his company when they were together.

★ ★ ★

They'd just arrived back at her flat from a theatre show in Glasgow and were having a meal when Beatrice breezed in. Gil guessed instantly that she had something to tell them. Although a good actress, she was hopeless at keeping her feelings hidden when off the stage.

'Why have you come up from Lockhart, Bea?' Rosalind was surprised.

'I knew you were both in Glasgow tonight and I wanted to see you together.' Beatrice gave an anxious look in Rosalind's direction, then turned to

Gil with what he took to be an appeal for support.

'It's this . . . Well, I'd like to be released from my contract at the Limelight.'

'What?' Rosalind was stunned.

'Why?' Gil knew this was a serious request.

'I didn't say anything, and I know I should have, but I thought you might not approve — I applied to the television company to go on a training course.'

'For what type of position?' Gil asked.

'As a potential floor manager.'

Gil leaned back in his chair.

'Oh, good, that sounds exactly right for you.'

Beatrice almost collapsed with relief.

'Oh, Gil, you really think so?'

'Will someone please tell me what's going on?' Rosalind demanded.

Gil turned to smile at her.

'It's the television version of theatre stage managing, something that Beatrice has been doing in the Limelight for months.'

Rosalind still looked confused.

'I made enquiries way back when the television company was in the theatre, and Ian Ramsay told me to apply. I was scared to mention it and didn't expect to be accepted, but I have, and Rosalind, I don't want to upset you . . . ' Beatrice ran out of steam.

Rosalind hesitated, but only for a moment, then gave Beatrice a hug.

'You haven't upset me. Taken me by surprise, yes, but if it's what you want, then that's what I want, too.'

'I'd never have achieved anything without your help!' Beatrice was near tears.

'Rubbish,' Rosalind said stoutly. 'No sentimentality, please! If it's all right with Gil, it's all right by me.'

'Oh, it will be all right with Gil. You two think as one now!' And Beatrice blew some kisses in the air and left the flat.

Gil looked over at Rosalind. Beatrice's comment gave him the perfect opening.

He waited until Rosalind returned to the table, then reached over and took her hand. The expression in her eyes was uncertain, but the flush on her cheeks was deeper.

'I noticed weeks ago that your engagement ring was no longer on your finger,' he began gently.

'I broke off the engagement. I didn't care enough for Nicol in the long run.'

He made no comment, just continued to gaze at her.

'I worried that you wouldn't think much of a woman who let down her fiancé,' she murmured.

So that was why she looked uncertain. He felt his heart leap. She did care what he thought of her!

'Actually, I thought he was the one who let you down, going off and leaving you behind,' he said.

'He met someone else in Canada and I don't blame him. I just didn't want to be with him. I discovered that my family and everyone and everything here are more important to me.' She lowered her head. 'I wasn't very true to him.'

'Nonsense to that.' He smiled and held on to her hand more firmly. 'Your marriage was just not meant to be. And you are the one person in the whole world that I put my trust in.'

He stroked her fingers.

'Everyone here is important to you?' he asked softly.

She nodded.

'I hope that includes me, because you mean everything to me, Rosalind.'

Rosalind had the strangest sensation that her bones were melting and yet her hand was still firmly in Gil's possession. She was powerless to take her gaze from his face.

'I hardly stop thinking of you all day.' The words seemed to come out of her mouth of their own volition, but she knew they came from her heart.

Almost as one they rose from the table and he took her in his arms.

'I said nothing before in case you were missing Nicol, but I've loved you for such a long time,' he murmured into her ear.

'Gil . . . I didn't know . . . didn't dare to hope once I realised how much you meant to me. I love you with all my heart. You've been my rock all these months. I can hardly wait for the weekends to come when I'll see you.' She laid her head on his shoulder.

'Leave Glasgow now, my dearest,' he said. 'Come to Lockhart — we'll be living there when we are married anyway.'

Rosalind lifted her head to look at him.

He gave her a tender smile.

'Yes, that is a proposal and I know I should go down on my knees, but I much prefer holding you in my arms.'

Rosalind gazed at his dear, loving face.

'I won't let you down, Gil. I know my heart is true to you.' She couldn't stop tears trickling down her cheeks.

He held her in his arms until she had quietened.

'How soon can you come?' he asked.

'I'll tell Andrew tomorrow that I'm leaving,' she promised. 'He'll be so happy for us.'

★　★　★

Her happiness cancelled out any trace of regret as Rosalind sealed the envelope containing her resignation letter. She'd been with Jardine House for thirteen years and had enjoyed working for Andrew. She'd tell him that now. She picked up the envelope and went into his office.

'Rosalind! The very person I wanted to see.' Andrew came round from behind his desk and planted a light kiss on her cheek. 'Do sit down.'

She took her usual chair with some misgivings. This was an unusual welcome from him.

He took his chair and literally beamed at her.

'I have some wonderful news for you. You remember we visited the gents' outfitters in Cathcart that was closing down? It's a good size and so well-appointed that I've decided to buy it, just to have a small suburban extension of Jardine House.'

'What a good idea.' She was genuinely pleased for him. 'Customers can't always get into the city to shop.'

'Exactly my thoughts. I'm going to transfer some of the Jardine House staff but, of course, I need a reliable manager.' He paused for effect. 'You've been a wonderful asset to me all the years you've worked here but never had a proper title to reflect that.'

She opened her mouth to speak. He must be stopped before he said any more.

'No, please let me finish. Rosalind, I want you to be the manager of our new Cathcart store.'

She found she couldn't speak. At long last a position she deserved, one she'd worked for and would have appreciated years ago. Now, it was the last thing she wanted.

'Lost your tongue?' Andrew was still beaming. 'I want you to start next month. I reckon it will probably take three months to get it up and running.'

'Andrew.' She finally managed to gather her thoughts and compose what she had to say. 'It's a great honour and I'm so flattered. I'd love to take it on, but . . . '

'No buts, Rosalind, I know you can do it. It's not as if you're going to Canada now, are you?' He pointed to her bare ring finger.

'No, that's all over, but I'm moving to Lockhart.'

'Lockhart? Whatever for?' His face was pale with shock.

It struck her that she couldn't tell him the real reason. Not yet. Livvy and Beatrice had to be the first to know.

'Livvy and Donald have bought a house there and, of course, there's Beatrice.' She left it at that. 'I've come to tell you that I'm leaving.'

'But what will you do there? You can't throw away your business talents!'

'I'll look for a job,' she said weakly, feeling terribly disloyal to him.

Andrew sat back in his chair, his face now like thunder.

'This is a terrible disappointment to me, Rosalind. And a shocking set-back to my plans for Cathcart.'

'I'm sorry, Andrew, I would have loved to take up the challenge, but I have other priorities.' It was the best she could do. She made to hand over her letter of resignation.

'If that's what I think it is, I don't want to see it. Give it straight to Muriel.'

Rosalind could see that any further words would only inflame the situation. She rose from her chair.

'Wait. If you insist on this mad idea, you'll need to find a good job in Lockhart.' He took out his wallet and extracted a business card.

'This is an old school friend of mine. Contact him. He'll know the best companies in the town.'

Rosalind thanked him, picked up the

card and slipped it into the pocket of her skirt.

★ ★ ★

'I felt like a traitor,' she said on the phone to Gil that evening.

'I can understand that, my love, but he'll understand when we tell him the real reason you're coming here.'

'Yes, he will. He thinks the world of you, Gil.'

'I hope he doesn't change that opinion.' He laughed. 'Anyway, I've been looking at the bookings and there are two weeks in the summer when we could get married. What do you think?'

'That would be wonderful, darling. And I might just find a temporary job until then.'

'Who did Andrew recommend in Lockhart?' Gil asked.

'Oh, I forgot to look. The card is still in my skirt pocket — hold on,' she said. 'It's a Mr Cunninghame, he's a solicitor with offices in Lockhart and Largs.'

There was a silence at the other end of the line.

'Gil?'

'We know who he is, Rosalind. He's the solicitor who handled the anonymous donation that saved the theatre.'

The connection hit Rosalind at once.

'Do you think he was acting for Andrew?'

'I can't think of anyone in Lockhart who could have afforded to make that size of donation. Andrew's rich, he's supported the theatre since you inherited it and, besides, he might have had Avril's career in mind.'

'Then we owe him.' Rosalind's voice was almost a whisper.

'Yes, we do,' Gil agreed at once. 'If it hadn't been for him, we'd have lost the theatre . . . and as a result we even might have lost each other.'

'He said it would take three months to get this new store up and running.'

'Maybe we should do this for him,' Gil replied.

'Just what I was thinking,' she said.

'But that will take until mid-summer.'

'I know, my darling.' His voice was low.

Next morning, Rosalind went straight to see Andrew.

'Would it be all right if I took on the job for the three months you mentioned?'

'My dear girl, it would be perfect.' He came round his desk and gave her a kiss on the cheek.

Although she was heartsore at not being with Gil sooner, it was their anonymous way of saying thank you to Andrew. They could never reveal that they knew he'd been their generous benefactor.

* * *

Kate Webster arrived in the middle of the night early in August. She was a healthy baby, much given to demanding attention using the power of her strong lungs.

Livvy had sailed through the birth and was in perfect health herself.

'Just in time, too, for me to get into my matron of honour outfit.' Livvy beamed at Rosalind.

'She's a bit tiny to be a bridesmaid, but we must find her something special to wear.' Beatrice gently stroked the baby's soft cheek.

'Can I carry her up the aisle?' Donald asked.

That would be just right, Rosalind thought. She had decided to ask Andrew to give her away. Not from any sense of gratitude to him, but just because he had no family of his own and she guessed he'd be pleased. And he was, and more — touched and proud.

Three weeks later, Rosalind took Andrew's arm and entered Lockhart Church. Although everyone connected with the Limelight had been invited, the pews were overflowing with Lockhart folk. Her heart warmed to the fact that so many had come to share their special day.

Gil turned round to watch her walk

towards him, the wonderful, gentle smile she loved so much matched by the tenderness in his eyes.

Although she didn't look at anyone else until she was by his side, she was aware of so many others.

Livvy took her bouquet, Beatrice arranged her train and Kate let out a wild gurgle as Donald took a seat in the front pew. Andrew relinquished her to Gil's care when they came to that part of the service, and Rosalind was somehow aware that he then took his seat beside Avril.

Rosalind wanted everyone to be happy today and hoped that maybe some time in the future, there would be a wedding there for Andrew and Avril, but only they could decide. As for Beatrice and Stuart, they seemed to be following ambitions, rather than hearts.

Then she was aware only of Gil as the marriage service united them for ever.

After the signing of the register, the vicar led them out of the vestry as he had an announcement to make before they proceeded down the aisle together.

'My dear friends, it has been a special joy to Gil and Rosalind to see you all here today. I hope you will all be able to rejoin us tomorrow.' He paused as a yell filled the air. He turned to Donald with a smile.

'Tomorrow that young lady, Katherine Webster, will be christened here. From the sound of her, she's already practising for a debut on the stage.'

The congregation laughed at his sally.

Next day, Rosalind held her god-daughter in her arms and promised to take care of her for life. Standing by the font, she was facing the pews, but saw only Gil. Her eyes sent him the same message. His nod transmitted an identical message to her.

Later that day, as they set off on their honeymoon, Rosalind asked the taxi driver to stop at the Limelight for a few minutes.

'Have you forgotten something?' Gil asked as she led him from the taxi.

She just smiled at him, unlocked the

theatre door, and then took his hand as they passed through the auditorium to the stage. She didn't let go until they were standing centre stage.

She turned him round to face the auditorium.

'This is where we met, where we fell in love, where our future lies,' she said.

'I know all that, my dearest. I haven't forgotten and nothing has changed,' he said.

'Oh, yes, it has.' She reached into her handbag and withdrew a sheet of paper. 'This is no longer a theatre belonging to the Forsyth sisters.'

Gil stared at her.

'Rosalind, what have you done?'

'I put a proposal to my sisters and they agreed at once. First, I bought out Livvy's share. You know that Donald wants to buy a second coach and employ a driver? Now, they can.'

'Beatrice has told us that she wants to work freelance, sometimes in the theatre, other times in television. She gladly sold me her share of the theatre,